SPIRIT TRAP

SPELLS FOR HIRE BOOK THREE

STEFON MEARS

Also by Stefon Mears

Cavan Oltblood Series
Half a Wizard
The Ice Dagger
Spells of Undeath

Spells for Hire
Devil's Shoestring
Zombie Powder
Spirit Trap
Dragon's Blood (coming December 2019)

The Rise of Magic
Magician's Choice
Sleight of Mind
Lunar Alchemy
Three Fae Monte
The Sphinx Principle

The Telepath Trilogy
Surviving Telepathy
Immoral Telepathy
Targeting Telepathy

Edge of Humanity
Caught Between Monsters
Hunting Monsters

Power City Tales
Not Quite Bulletproof
No Money in Heroism

Devil's Night
Portal-Land, Oregon
Stealing from Pirates
Fade to Gold
With a Broken Sword
Twice Against the Dragon
The House on Cedar Street
Sudden Death
On the Edge of Faerie
Confronting Legends (Spells & Swords Vol. 1)
Uncle Stone Teeth and Other Macabre Poems
The Patreon Collection, Vol. 1-4 (Vol. 5, coming soon)

Published by Thousand Faces Publishing, Portland, Oregon

http://1kfaces.com

Front cover image © Dmitrijs Bindemanis | Dreamstime.com

ISBN: 978-1-948490-20-7

SPIRIT ✝ TRAP

SPELLS FOR HIRE | BOOK THREE

AUTHOR'S NOTE

Spells for Hire stories take place in a world that is very like our own, but is not our own.

Thus, you might be able to visit some of the locations described in this book, such as the Witch's Castle in Forest Park. Others, however, have been fictionalized or invented whole cloth, like Gripper. Where I have fictionalized or invented, I have tried to maintain that unique Portland vibe.

In much the same way, religions such as Vodou, Candomblé and Shugendō exist in this world, as do other practices such as Hoodoo. I have done substantial research in my attempts to keep my portrayals true to the spirit of those beliefs and practices. I have, however, taken liberties for dramatic purposes. I hope that devotees of those religions and practices will forgive any mistakes I have made.

1

———————

FAR AS HEATH CYR WAS CONCERNED, NOTHING SHORT OF A NATURAL disaster was a good reason to get out of bed before noon.

Right now it was not quite ten a.m.

Heath, by all rights, should have been fast asleep between the soft cotton sheets of his California king. Preferably with Nariko, his girlfriend, naked and curled up beside him. His tuxedo cat, Dr. John, tucked into a tight little purring ball on Heath's chest.

Nariko, alas, was camping out at Mount Hood. Something to do with her Shugendō practice. Heath hadn't quite followed the symbology of her explanation, though. Some things just must not translate right from Japanese.

Still, he understood that mountains played an important role in her magic, and he understood that this trip was important to her. It was also something she had to do alone.

Dr. John was outside, likely harassing field mice that had the misfortune of finding they'd left Forest Park for the surrounding neighborhoods.

And Heath, to his current dismay, was not in bed.

He was fully dressed. Leather boat shoes. Navy blue cargo shorts, with all the extra pockets stuffed full of little helpers he might need, depending on how the day went. A couple of them were mojo bags, but the others, supplies in ready-to-use packets.

For a shirt, he wore a pale blue, feather-light button-up, with short sleeves. Tucked into the breast pockets, a couple of things he hoped he wouldn't need, but kept on his person whenever he was in public. Just in case.

Heath wasn't expecting trouble, but his grandmother always said: "Trouble's not a guest anyone *invites*."

And if he needed anything else, that was why he wore a black canvas backpack over one shoulder, containing just about any tools a conjure man like himself might need to deal with any uninvited trouble.

More than two solid hours before noon, and here Heath was entering Powell's City of Books. Not because of a natural disaster, but for something that prove more personally significant.

Heath had to meet a client.

This particular client was a woman on the Trail Blazers' stunt team. This went well, it could open up a whole new client base for Heath.

And if the Trail Blazers themselves started coming to him for readings or spells? Well, NBA players weren't exactly hard up for cash.

Maybe Heath could even become the official root doctor for an NBA team...

Still. Powell's was not the place he would have chosen to meet a client.

By preference, he would have liked someplace with a veneer of privacy. A table in a public park would have been good. Riverfront Park maybe, or Forest Park, or *any* of the little parks that dotted the little city. Sitting in the morning sunshine at a sidewalk bistro or café might have been even better. A ready source of caffeine, and a chance to enjoy some of the last clear days of the year.

It was September now, and in Portland, Oregon, that meant the rains would be back any day. If Heath had to be conscious and outside at this unholy hour, he might as well at least enjoy the weather.

But no. The client wanted Powell's.

On the one hand, Heath could understand it. A woman, meeting a strange man for the first time. A man she only knew by reputation. The safe way to play was to meet him at one of the busiest places she could, without setting it up to have to buy him lunch or something.

But she could have at least agreed to a reasonable hour.

Heath was tired, and in crowded places that sometimes triggered his old Manhattan instincts.

Like right now.

Three steps inside the building, and already he felt the grimace start. The tension through his shoulders. His elbows jutting out a little more, ready to clear a path if he needed them to. His stride already tightened into the swift gait of the Manhattanite.

This was just the magazine section — a room bigger than a lot of other bookstores Heath could name — but it was near the checkout, where already dozens of tourists were pouring over the Powell's branded merchandise.

They were inside one of the biggest bookstores in the western United States — if not in fact the western hemisphere — and instead of going through any one of the four floors of books available in the *whole city block* of floorspace, they were huddled by the cashiers. Looking at bags and tee shirts, drink bottles and more.

Heath practically growled.

Caffeine was not going to be enough. He'd need chocolate.

And if this client was late, he'd double his fee.

Heath made his way to the coffee shop — without needing to elbow anyone, which was probably for the best.

He didn't need to hand over his backpack at the front counter, either, because of a little *ignore-me* charm that kept anyone in authority from noticing it.

Wasn't as though Heath was going to steal anything.

The coffee shop at Powell's was bigger than a number of the local bistros he could have named.

Maybe that was a good thing. More observers meant a better chance at more curiosity.

The coffee shop had some small, mismatched tables with two or four chairs, but more floor space was dedicated to great, long tables where groups would have to share space. And along the outside walls — glass, of course, so passersby could see all the fun people were having inside — a rail table with plenty of stools.

Support pillars and twelve-foot bookshelves separated tables and gave people the pretense of privacy. But the noise level belied it.

Only a few minutes before ten a.m., and already every table was in use by a diverse cross-section of humanity, from the students and hipster kids to the business-suit types through the old folks on their outings. All talking and laughing, debating and arguing, drinking and eating, using the wifi and working on laptops or tablets or phones.

Some of them even had books.

Yes, at least there'd be plenty of witnesses. Some of them might grow curious enough to ask questions, after the client left. Maybe even try a reading...

"Excuse me," a contralto woman's voice said, from behind Heath. "Are you Heath Cyr?"

Good. She wasn't running late.

That little detail helped Heath plaster something close to a real smile on his face when he turned around.

And found himself looking right over the head of his client.

Heath was only about six feet tall, but this woman had to be more than a foot shorter than he was.

Fortunately for her, she had the looks and personality to make herself seem to take more space than she did.

Some people, they seem to shrink when they're out in public. As though they take up less space than physics says is possible. But this woman, she was one of the opposite types. Even looking down to see her, Heath almost felt as though she was his height.

She had bright green, eyes. Almost Kelly green, and smiling. And the face surrounding them was spattered with more freckles than a body her size should have been able to hold. But then, the freckles went with the cascading red hair that hung down past her shoulders.

She wore a red halter top over black yoga pants, and she wore the outfit like a fitness model. Tiny black purse with a Trail Blazers logo hung off her shoulder.

"I'm Heath," he said, holding out his hand to shake. "You must be Cynthia."

She nodded with a smile, and her handshake showed a grip that Heath took to mean she was used to getting challenged.

Heath didn't offer a challenge. If she had to "win" the handshake, he had no problem with that.

"Didn't think it would be this full before noon," she said with a grimace. "Think we'll be able to get a table?"

"Oh," Heath said with a wink, "I think one will clear up for us."

Heath strode toward the four-top in the middle of the coffee shop. The best table. Solid wood, scuffed and lacquered, with initials carved into it and graffiti marking it. Good strong chairs around it.

As he started walking, the four suited businessmen currently occupying it suddenly all shook themselves out of their conversation. Like maybe they were all late for the same big meeting.

They grabbed their dishes and stepped away from the table...

...just exactly in time for Heath to sit down without breaking stride and sling his backpack onto an empty chair. Ahead of two other people who had jumped like they wanted to claim the table for themselves. Maybe had been waiting to do so.

Heath looked up to where Cynthia was still standing. Huge, self-satisfied smile on his face.

The businessmen never looked at Heath, nor he at them. He didn't know them. Had no idea where they were off to. But they didn't matter. What did matter was that, before Heath left his house, he'd worked a *find-my-spot* charm to ensure that the perfect table would open up for him just when he needed it.

Extravagant? Yes.

More effort than it was worth? Normally, yes.

But meeting a client someplace busy?

The slack-jawed surprise on her face made it worthwhile.

HEATH HAD TO SHOO AWAY TWO ATTEMPTS TO "BORROW" CHAIRS FROM his table while Cynthia was in line to get them coffee. But Heath planned on keeping this table after he was done with his client, and he wasn't sure how many seats he'd need.

So he sat in the heavy wooden chair, warmed by the butt of the businessman who'd been sitting in it mere seconds before vacating it for Heath. And he wiped down the lacquered surface of the table.

And then he just closed his eyes for a moment.

First, he let himself enjoy the hubbub. Any coffee shop this busy was noisy with conversations and laughter and shrill moments. Scrapes of utensils on plates, or cups set down too hard, or the scrape of chairs across the floor.

And overflowing as the Powell's coffee shop was that morning, Heath could almost pretend he was a teenager again, back on 52nd street in Manhattan.

A simple pleasure, and one he didn't often get in a town as laid back as Portland.

So Heath savored it. The press and noise of humanity over the suction of the espresso machine and the grind of the coffee makers.

Heath made himself hear everything he could.

Then he focused on his sense of smell. Some three or four varieties of coffee, plus another six of baked goods. And, if he wasn't mistaken, a little eggs and bacon as well.

Good. Good.

When Heath was sure he'd gotten every sound and smell he could, he calibrated. Now that he had them, he needed to tune them out. Focus in until he could hear the sound of his own breaths again. Slow and deep. The thump of his own steady heartbeat.

Good.

Then, Heath opened his eyes. Scanned the room to make sure he didn't spot any trouble. He hadn't smelled any, but it was best to be sure.

Then, with his eyes still moving among the diverse crowd of the coffee shop, he let his hands dig into his backpack, where it rested on the seat beside him.

He pulled out his favorite pack of playing cards. Favorite for reading, anyway. It was an old deck. Red. Bicycle brand. One he'd picked up more than a decade ago now. The first cards he'd learned to read with. They were worn with age, and thousands of shufflings.

By the time he'd shuffled and cut them seven times, sitting at the table that day, Cynthia arrived. She set down their coffee, along with a Greek yogurt with nuts for her, and a chocolate muffin for Heath.

"You really do read playing cards," she said.

"Well," Heath said with a shrug, "a good diviner can read just about anything. But I'm best with the cards or the cowries. And most people prefer—"

"You read the cowries?" She blinked, then leaned closer. "Do you have them with you?"

Heath had to admit the question surprised him. Most white people hardly seemed to know what cowrie shells were, much less that anyone could read the future with them.

"No," Heath said, shaking his head. "This is their day to get clean, to make sure my set is clear of any ... habits or such, if you will. Would you rather reschedule and get a cowrie reading instead?"

"No," she said through a long breath as she sat back. "No, I'd rather get the reading today. But if we do this again—"

"Believe me," Heath said with perfect sincerity, "I will have no trouble remembering in the future that you prefer the cowries." His turn to lean forward a little. "Truth to tell, I prefer them when I read for myself."

That got a smile out of her, and she seemed to relax a little. She sipped at her coffee, while Heath squared the deck and set it in the middle of the table.

"So," he said, "you know how this goes then?"

"Yes," she said with a frown, "and no. I've had readings before, but only with tarot cards."

"Never touch the stuff," Heath said with a grin, and sipped his own coffee. "To me, tarot has too much baggage. I like the pure simplicity of playing cards."

Cynthia nodded. Looked unsure again.

"So," Heath said, setting down his cup. "I have trouble believing a pretty girl like you needs love advice. So is it career stuff then?"

"No," she said, and her tone got crisp. Every bit as businesslike as Heath had ever heard from a client before. "No, I'm at a crossroads right now in my life, and I need to figure out which way to go. I need a general reading, with some advice to it, if you don't mind."

"Not at all," Heath said, then pursed his lips, pushed them around, and said, "Have to say, though, that we can only go so far with a reading in public. You're likely to hold back a little, or want me to hold back on what I say. And I'm only going to lay out so many cards here."

"Don't hold anything back," she said. "And Lilac said you're good at talking around issues, where discretion is needed."

Ah, Lilac. A little blonde slip of a hipster girl who favored a retro 60s look. Heath's first client in Portland, and to this day still his steadiest.

"All right," Heath said, with a shrug. "You want the twelve-card reading then, or the full fifty-four?"

"Don't you mean fifty-two?"

"Nope," Heath said with a shake of his head. "For this style reading, the jokers stay in."

Cynthia bit her lower lip. "How long would that take?"

"A good two hours, if it's going to be done right. And it would cost a little more than Lilac probably—"

"The fifty-four. And she told me what your more involved readings cost." Cynthia patted her purse significantly.

"Well, all right then."

Two hours was what it took, all right.

Heath and Cynthia both went through two cups of coffee, though Heath was too busy talking to eat more than half his muffin.

Poor girl was up against it all right.

One, her dad was sick. Possibly with cancer. But he was insisting she not come home to Seattle. That she had her own life to take care of, and if things turned for the worse, there'd be plenty of time for her to come visit then. She needed to know if she really did have time.

Two, there were harassment issues at the gym where she worked as a personal trainer (apparently the stunt team gig was part-time). One of the other trainers had been more than a little inappropriate with some of his clients. This was the sort of thing that might take just him down, or might bring down the whole gym, and she needed to know which.

Three, her boyfriend had gotten distant. Started working later. Missing date nights. Not too often, but enough to set the hairs on the back of her neck to standing up. She needed to know if work really was just that busy for him, or if another woman was getting the time she wasn't getting.

Four, her landlord had gotten slow to repair some problems with her sink and her heater. She was worried that he was trying to get rid of her, so he could spike the rent for the next tenant. And the way the rental market was, she worried about what she'd be able to find, if he was.

Those were just the big problems. They didn't count the three or four of five (Heath had lost count) smaller problems Heath bumped up against in the course of such a detailed reading.

She hadn't raised any of those issues before Heath dealt out the cards. They came up as Heath made observations about what he was seeing. At first, she'd been close-lipped, worried that he was doing some kind of fortune teller cold-reading con.

But as Heath kept going. Started getting into details and issues and angles she hadn't mentioned, she started opening up.

For example, Heath had spotted the trouble in her love life first thing, and mentioned the symptoms and the cause (sadly, there *was* another woman in the picture) before she said a word.

And the problem with her father had been right there too. Both those issues hung tightest over her, to the point that she finally had to admit that she'd spoken to both her boyfriend (soon to be ex-) and her mother before coming in to meet Heath.

By the end of the reading, Heath was, at least, able to give her some good news.

First, her dad wasn't likely to die before next summer. Heath had to admit he wasn't sure why next summer was the date coming up, and that it didn't mean he'd die next summer. Just that, from what Heath was reading, her father was *likely* to live through the new year and at least past spring.

Next, and this came out of one of those problems she considered minor, Cynthia had the chance to invest in a gym opening up in the Portland suburb of Tigard, but it would mean quitting her job and investing all her money in it.

Of all the things Heath read for her in the cards, the *go* sign for that opportunity was the loudest and clearest. She might need to move, and dump her boyfriend, and leave her main job, but she had a good prospect on the horizon, and her dad wasn't likely to die before her new venture got off the ground.

So all told, by the time Cynthia left that table smack dab in the middle of the coffee shop at Powell's City of Books, she was smiling and looked to be feeling a little better about life.

As for Heath, he'd spotted at least a dozen interested observers. Watching the reading. Talking in stage whispers to their friends about the man who had just given a "psychic" reading for such a pretty woman, who paid him with a plain white envelope of cash and gushed her thanks before she left.

Heath knew what they were saying. Wondering if he was a scammer. Wondering how much money he made. Wondering if maybe, just maybe, he was the real thing.

But Heath let them wonder. One of them might be willing to ask. Take a chance. Maybe today. Maybe some other day.

And when they found out just how accurate Heath could be with his playing cards, well, a whole new stream of clients would open up.

And if they didn't, this was still a good place to sit and wait for Colin to finish his book shopping.

Plus, the casual observers might not be the only source of additional work to come out of this morning's reading.

Cynthia got her recommendation from Lilac. Lilac would ask about the reading. And Lilac would be sure to point out the spells and charms Heath could provide that would help with the landlord, the new business venture, and especially the soon-to-be-ex-boyfriend. Talk about the good Heath had done Lilac over the years with his conjure work.

Heath didn't mention any spells or charms himself, of course. Might have sounded too much like using the reading to get people to buy something else.

Heath didn't play that game. Thought it diminished the fine art of divination.

Heath gave fair readings for fair money. Any spells or other help people wanted, they had to ask for on their own.

Once Cynthia was gone, Heath set the deck in the center of the table, tore off a bit of muffin and tossed it into his mouth, and savored it.

Yes, even Heath had to admit, this had been a gig worth getting up early for.

Heath was just finishing up his coffee when he heard Colin's approach.

"Heath!"

Never the subtle one, Colin. He was the kind of guy who lived in a state of exuberance.

Heath turned with a smile to see what excited his friend this time.

Colin was wearing what Heath had come to think of as Colin's uniform: worn, paint-stained jeans over sneakers that looked on the verge of giving up the ghost. A heavy metal tee shirt — for yet another band Heath had never heard of, this one called "Kyng" — and his fine blond hair streaming halfway down his back.

He was also carrying quite a stack of books.

"Heath!" Colin said again, stopping to pull out a chair with his foot and giving Heath a smile so big it could only have meant one thing.

"Who is she?" Heath said, smiling. "Or is it a he this time?"

"She this time, and oh my god, Heath." Colin mimed fainting back in his chair.

He also dropped his books on the table, which was solid enough not to do more than thump, when by all rights the sheer weight should have produced a minor earthquake.

"Go on," Heath said, shaking his head and setting down his empty cup.

"Five feet of heaven," Colin said, eyes still closed. "She has this coppery red hair that only comes down just past her shoulders, but just looks like it was spun by angels from the light of the setting sun."

Colin opened his eyes and wiggled his eyebrows. "She also has these amazing legs. Not to mention the most lickable abs I've ever seen on a woman."

Heath made a show of closing his eyes and putting one hand to his forehead. "And her name was ... Cynthia?"

"How'd you..."

Heath opened his eyes, but held back the smile. Instead he popped a piece of chocolate muffin in his mouth.

"Your client?"

Heath nodded. Tore the last of his muffin into two small bites.

"What'd she want to know?"

"If she'd ever find love," Heath said. "I told her to watch for a skinny white boy carrying books that weighed more than he did."

Colin snickered like a cartoon dog. "Fine, don't tell me."

"As though I'd ever tip what a client wanted to talk about." Then Heath made a show of looking around the crowd. "Of course, if she wanted true discretion, she'd have wanted to meet somewhere else."

"If she'd wanted true discretion," a smooth, deep voice said, "she'd have gone to a better reader."

Heath frowned and turned his attention to the man stepping

around one of the twelve-foot bookshelves. A man about a decade older than Heath. A man who looked like he should have been starring in rap videos. He stood just under six feet tall, so just a little shorter than Heath, but he probably weighed three times as much.

Calling this man fat might have been accurate, but it wouldn't have begun to cover it. He was offensive lineman big, with plenty of muscle under all that fat.

He wore a tailored royal blue suit, with a black shirt and tie, a good combination for his dark chocolate skin. Bald head so smooth it gleamed.

Diamond tie tack. Diamond cufflinks. Three gold rings. One cup of coffee.

"DeAndre McDaniels," Heath said.

And here the day had been going so well.

THE ESPRESSO MACHINE STARTED TO HISS, AS THOUGH OBJECTING TO the presence of DeAndre McDaniels — gangbanger turned conjure man — in so fine an establishment as the Powell's City of Books coffee shop.

Heath liked that thought, but he knew it wasn't true. Just a matter of timing.

Goodness knew the rest of the establishment didn't seem to object to the man's presence. Animated conversation and consumption continued apace all around the crowded café.

"Heath Cyr," DeAndre rumbled. "Or should I call you Twilight?"

Twilight. A nickname, and one that might have been kind of cool, if not for those vampire books. But Heath had no say in the matter. People had started calling him "Twilight" not long after he set up shop in Portland a few years back.

Some called him that because his clients used to find him in Riverfront Park, around dusk.

Some called him that because, as Colin put it, Heath's magic was "neither bright as day, nor dark as night."

Some, though, called Heath Twilight because Heath didn't have the pale white Irish skin of his mother, nor the blue-black Deep South skin of his father. But somewhere in the middle.

Somewhere in the middle. Like so many things about Heath.

And if he had to bet how DeAndre meant it, he was betting on skin tone. Which just soured Heath's mood all the more.

"What are you doing here, DeAndre? Hoping to find a primer on magic? *Hoodoo for the Chronically Inept* maybe?"

"Is that a real book?" Colin asked quickly. "Because I've never understood how the hell you guys make a bunch of herbs and roots do magic."

Colin was one to talk. The occult community called him "Weird Colin" because he managed to get obscure 1970s self-help books with terrible titles to perform real, powerful magic.

"Look, truce. Okay?" DeAndre removed one of his gold rings. Placed it on the table in front of Heath. "If I make a move you don't like before I leave, I give you permission to take that and do to me what you will."

Colin whistled.

Probably not as big a gesture as DeAndre was trying to make it look. Probably not one of the rings he was noted for always wearing — which would have more value as a magical link. More likely a ring he just picked up or had bought for him sometime in the last hour, and put on just for show.

Still, it was a gesture. And DeAndre *had* worn it, and explicitly offered it as a link. So it was better than nothing.

And Heath wouldn't learn anything if he told DeAndre to fuck off, tempting as it might be.

Worse, that might start a showdown. And Heath didn't want another fight right now.

It had been nearly two solid weeks since Heath's last magical fight. And the way the summer was going, he didn't expect that happy streak to last.

But that didn't mean Heath would make things easy on DeAndre.

"All right," Heath said. "I accept your offer, and I ask Damballah to witness it."

DeAndre blinked. Took a half-step back, one hand raised as though warding off a blow.

Heath locked his eyes on DeAndre's.

"Damballah," Heath said, only just loud enough for Colin and DeAndre to hear his prayer over the background chatter, "I ask You to witness and assure this man's offer of truce. And if it is insincere, great Damballah, I ask You to make him suffer for his deception. As thanks, I offer You honey."

Heath swept his remaining muffin and its crumbs onto a napkin. With his other hand, he dug a small bottle of honey out of his backpack, and squeezed a slow stream into a snake shape on the small, white plate, dedicating the act to Damballah.

A cool feeling of peace settled into Heath's stomach. Damballah wasn't a vengeful Lwa like Kalfou or one of the Barons, but He was just. And He saw right through bullshit.

Heath smiled at DeAndre as he closed the honey bottle and slipped it back into his backpack.

"Trusting sort, aren't you?" DeAndre said, emphasizing the *aren't* as though he'd been practicing phonics or something.

"If my body floated to the surface of the Willamette River tomorrow, you'd be one of the top three suspects."

"Fair enough," DeAndre said with a considering frown. Maybe trying to guess the other two suspects.

"You've spoken to me three times since I moved to Portland. Every one of them was a threat."

"Fair enough," DeAndre said again, a little firmer, and with a nod for emphasis. "Not that any of them did me any good. May I sit?"

Heath nodded to the open chair.

DeAndre looked Heath over as he sat. Judging his clothes maybe, or his lack of jewelry. But Heath knew he and DeAndre had lived very different lives. And Heath's hadn't included jail time.

"How you stay so skinny," DeAndre said as Heath finished his muffin, "eating all that chocolate, is a thing I will never understand."

"There's a lot about me you'll never understand, DeAndre."

"Hey," he said, holding up a calming hand. "Truce. Remember?"

Heath raised an eyebrow. DeAndre knew damned well what Heath was waiting for.

"Fine," DeAndre said with a nod. Then spoke louder for what he said next. And Heath had to admit, the man had a voice for projection.

"I was only giving you shit. Everyone knows you're *aces* with the cards and cowries, Heath Cyr."

"Thank you," Heath said.

Colin waved one hand in the air between Heath and DeAndre.

"Oh, excuse me," DeAndre said, turning in his chair and smiling at Colin. "Didn't see you there behind all those books." He nodded a greeting. "Weird Colin."

"DeAndre," Colin said, nodding back. "That offer of truce go for me too?"

DeAndre's eyes rounded wide in shock. But that was probably nothing to the shocked look on Heath's face. He knew he felt his jaw drop, and Heath's jaw didn't drop easily.

"It does," DeAndre said. "Didn't think you of all people would be spoiling for a fight."

"I'm not," Colin said with a simple shrug. "I hate fighting. I just wanted to make sure you're not going to pull a trick on me while you're here."

"In front of Heath Cyr?" DeAndre chuckled and shook his head. "I'm good at what I do, but if there's a trickier mother fucker in the five-oh-three, I haven't met him."

"Truce, and now a compliment," Heath said. "Am I supposed to believe this is a social call?"

"Why not?" DeAndre said with a smile. He did have a good, strong set of white teeth. He set down his coffee cup. "We're both conjure men. And we're both *brothers*. Seems to me we might be better off finding some common ground. Sticking together, given the number of Latinos around here doing Palo Mayombe, Santeria—"

"Quimbanda," Heath added, significantly.

DeAndre met Heath's eyes. Both men knew who Heath meant.

Vizinha. The gorgeous Brazilian woman who had been *the* major player in the local conjure-rootworker scene. Until she and Heath ended up at crossed purposes over a client ... just about two weeks ago.

Heath hadn't seen her since. Didn't know if she was looking for revenge, licking her wounds, or just recovering from a very bad decision on her part.

She'd managed to trap the American avatar of male sex appeal. And tried to keep him to herself.

Heath had probably freed *her* that night, as much as the avatar.

"So you see what I mean," DeAndre said with another smile.

"I get along just fine with the *brujos* and *curanderos* and at least some of the *Paleros* and *Santeros*." Heath shrugged. "If you're not, maybe that's on you."

"Yeah," Colin said. "Not everything is about race, you know."

"Easy words for a white man to say," DeAndre said.

"But in *this* case," Heath said, "accurate." Heath shook his head. "And I'm betting you know that."

Heath gave DeAndre a look of diminishing patience.

"You're a hard man," DeAndre said. "Should have been a gangster."

"If you were serious about a social call," Heath said, "maybe even burying the hatchet, you'd have done it someplace more public. Like Gripper. And you'd've bought me a beer."

Gripper, the one Portland bar frequented only by those in the magical know. No one else was likely to even realize it was a bar, much less open to the public.

If it happened at Gripper, the whole magical community of the greater Portland area would know about it in a day or less.

"At the very least," Colin added, "you'd've wanted Nariko to witness. Because if anything happens to Heath, *she's* the one you'll have to worry about."

True. Heath's girlfriend just happened to be the toughest person Heath knew, when it came to straight up magical combat.

"So I'll ask again, DeAndre," Heath said. "What do you want?"

DeAndre let out a sigh that almost seemed to deflate him. He looked about. Nervous? Or an act? He leaned forward. Spoke his next words softly.

"I'm in a bind, and I don't see a way out." DeAndre closed his eyes, and his next words sounded pained.

"I'm here to ask you for help."

TWO TABLES AWAY, SOMEONE BURST OUT LAUGHING. NOT AT DEANDRE'S admission, though. Just part of the press of background chatter surrounding Heath, Colin and DeAndre here in the coffee shop at Powell's City of Books.

Joining the conversation, the hiss of the espresso machine, the whir and grind of the coffee makers, the clatter of dishware. Even the faint sounds of traffic from the streets on the other side of the glass window walls here at the corner of the building.

All that, Heath could hear clearly.

So why didn't he trust what his ears told him DeAndre had just said?

"DeAndre," Heath said slowly, "I'm not trying to put you on the spot, but I'm going to need you to say that again. Just to make sure I heard you right."

"You heard me right," he said, his deep voice gaining a touch of angry growl.

"Can't have," Heath said, shaking his head slowly. "All the shit you've given me over the years, and now you're here to ask for help? No way I heard that right."

"Damn it!" DeAndre swore loudly, then lowered his voice again. And his next words did come out a growl. "I said I need your help. Want me to beg for it?"

"No," Heath said slowly. "But I do want you to explain why you are sitting here, asking *me* for help, instead of someone you might call a friend. Maybe José."

José Rodrigo-Montoya. A *Palero* that DeAndre seemed to be on good terms with. Or at the very least, a *Palero* that Heath had seen DeAndre drinking with at Gripper, apparently on good terms.

A *Palero*...

Heath raised an eyebrow.

DeAndre shook his head.

"No," he said. "José and I are still on pretty good terms. But, well, you know what it's like, working the darker side of the street." DeAndre's turn to raise an eyebrow. "Or maybe you don't?"

"I'm not exactly shiny white and clean," Heath said. "I just don't play with those forces nonstop like you guys do."

"Then you should know that the last thing I can do is go to someone like José for help. Show a guy like him weakness..."

"...and he uses it against you," Heath finished for him, thinking about his uncle. Heath's uncle was just the sort of man to use a moment of weakness against a so-called friend. "Great at picking friends, aren't you?"

"Heath," Colin said, then leaned in to whisper. "Come on, man. The guy's obviously suffering if he's willing to come to you for help. Maybe hear him out?"

Heath almost snapped at Colin, but checked the words before they slipped past his lips. Snorted a bit of a laugh.

"All right," Heath said. "Why don't you tell me what the problem is, and then maybe we'll see if I'm willing to help you out."

DeAndre turned and looked significantly at Colin.

Oh. So DeAndre was counting on a certain amount of discretion then?

"You know," Heath said, "Colin's going to spread the word that you came to me for help, whether I help you or not."

"I've already texted Nariko," Colin added with a shrug. Then Colin took a good look at DeAndre's expression at hearing those words and said, "why don't I get you guys some refills?"

Colin slipped away from the table quickly.

"Price of talking in a public place," Heath said without a trace of apology in his voice.

"Fair enough," DeAndre said through a sigh. "If it gets your help, it's worth it."

"So, what's the problem?"

"Do you know how I got my start on the path of conjure?"

Heath shook his head.

"I was on the inside, doing a dime for murder." DeAndre shrugged. "I was a 'banger then. Anyway, while on the inside, I met a man named Papa Dusk. He saw that I had some potential inside me that he didn't see in any of the other inmates."

Heath rolled in his lips to keep from saying anything. He wasn't sure he'd trust the opinion of anyone who called himself Papa Dusk. But then, Heath's own path to conjure had involved almost getting sacrificed to Baron Samedi by his own uncle. So maybe Heath had no room to cast stones here.

"Well, Papa Dusk, he taught me a lot. Got me started on the ways of rootwork, and all the things we could do with even just the stuff we could gather on the inside."

"I take it you don't mean the right plants?"

DeAndre shook his head. "The other stuff. What we could do with paper and ink made from bodily fluids. That sort of thing. I'm sure you can piece it together."

Heath nodded. Lots of power in personal effluvia.

"Anyway, once I started getting my mojo on, prison life got a hell of a lot better. But the one thing I was failing at every time was trying to get any help with my sentence."

"Really?" Heath said, more than a little surprised. Spells affecting lawyers, judges and court cases were staples of most conjure practice.

"I know," DeAndre said through a sigh. "I still suck at it. Personally, I think Papa Dusk whammied me to keep me from succeeding on that topic."

Heath felt cold realization wash over his face, as Colin sat back down with fresh cups of coffee for all three of them.

DeAndre glanced at Colin.

Colin held up three fingers, even though Heath doubted Colin had ever been a boy scout.

"I solemnly swear," Colin said, "I will keep the details of what you talk about among the three of us only. I will not bring up any of it with anyone, apart from the general points that you came to Heath for help, and that it had to do with the way you guys do magic."

DeAndre looked at Heath.

"That's the best you'll get from him," Heath said, still waiting for DeAndre to confirm what Heath suspected, "and he's good about keeping his word."

DeAndre nodded.

"So, Papa Dusk told me that there was some strong counter-magic keeping me from shortening my sentence or getting an early release."

"Go on." Heath could almost taste his pulse.

"There was only one way."

The foreplay was getting old.

"Who'd you make a deal with?" Heath said. "And what did you offer?"

"There was this guard. Worst kind of corrupt. Abused the prisoners, and I mean everyone he could get away with. And different kinds of abuse, you know what I'm telling you?"

Heath wasn't sure he did, but he was equally sure he didn't want to ask. He asked the more germane question instead.

"You sacrificed him?"

"Held the shiv myself. We did the working with his heart's blood. Papa Dusk covered it up."

"That's not Hoodoo," Heath said. "Not any kind of conjure I know. Darkest conjure stuff I've heard of involves black cat bone, and that's bad enough. Takes a sick individual to boil a living cat. But human sacrifice?" Heath shook his head. "Need a religion involved for something that sick."

"Figured that much out myself," DeAndre said, "though not until a couple of years later."

"What's all this have to do with your problem?" Colin asked.

"Simple," Heath said. "DeAndre here sacrificed a human being as part of an offering, and got his freedom as part of the deal, right?"

"Got released only two days later," DeAndre said. "Chain of evidence issue. Officially, anyway."

"And I'm betting that there was a time limit on this deal. Maybe ten years?"

"Seven," DeAndre said, looking at Heath with a little more respect.

"You got shorted," Heath said, maybe just a little brusque. "And I'm also betting that whatever Papa Dusk got out of the bargain got tied into *your* paying the price, right?"

DeAndre nodded, looking more and more impressed.

"Now the bill's come due, and a whole lot of things are crashing down on your head. And you can't use your own magic to dig yourself out of it, because you were part of the deal that made it happen in the first place."

"Tried everything I could think of and a few things I made up."

"Sucks to be you," Heath said.

DeAndre's eyes got wider than the rim of his coffee cup. "You're not going to help me?"

Colin looked just as surprised.

"Don't know yet," Heath said. "First thing I need to know, who got the offering?"

"This demon named Rochonzon. I've tried digging around. Seems to be big with the Western Ceremonialists, especially the Crowley-heads. What do they call themselves? Thelemites?"

"Big with the chaos magick set too," Colin said, off-handed. "They treat it like a patron."

"Worse and worse," Heath said. "What about this Papa Dusk? Where's he these days?"

"Gone," DeAndre said. "He got released before I did. Haven't heard from him since."

"Might be good, might be bad." Heath shook his head. "You understand, I can talk to this thing. And if there's a loophole, maybe I can find it. But you made a deal. I'm not risking my own rep among the spirit world by helping you *break* a deal."

"I just want you to help me survive it."

Heath took a long pull from his coffee cup, and almost spat it out. All the good coffee they had in this place, and Colin got him that hazelnut crap he loved so much.

Colin didn't even have the grace to look apologetic when Heath glared at him.

Heath set down his coffee cup.

"Okay," Heath said, rubbing his hands together. "One more thing before I decide."

"Anything you need to know," DeAndre said, leaning forward.

"Now," Heath said slowly, "you're here under a promise of truce, so I'm pretty sure you're not setting me up. I figure you know better than to cross Damballah."

DeAndre held up his right hand like was on the witness stand. "I swear. Everything I've told you sitting here at this table today has been true."

"And you look like you mean it." Heath rolled his pursed lips around. "But before I can believe it, I have to be *sure*. Normally I'd take a look at you through my spirit eyes, but I'm thinking you're putting up a front right now, so you don't start attracting vultures."

"I am," DeAndre said, more hesitation in his voice now. "I'll take it down if I have to, but—"

Heath stopped him with an upraised hand. With his other hand he pushed forward his deck of cards.

"Shuffle them three times."

DeAndre nodded, and shuffled those cards so fast and sure that he might have been a poker dealer in his spare time.

DeAndre squared the deck and set it back on the table.

"One card now," Heath said, addressing the deck. "Tell me what's up."

Heath cut the deck and looked at the card he cut.

"Let me guess," DeAndre said, sounding defeated. "Ace of Spades?"

"Worse," Heath said, showing him the card that was cut. The Jack of Spades.

"Why is that worse?" Colin asked.

"Jack's just an errand boy," DeAndre said with a grimace. "Answers to the king and queen, and in this case the ace."

"Worse than that," Heath said through a sigh, answering from his gut, where all the truest divinations came from. "In this case, the jack's hunted by the king and the ace. Not sure about the queen."

"Will you help me?" DeAndre asked.

Simple words, and somehow those bass tones of his managed to sound like a little boy who just found out there really was a monster under his bed.

"All right," Heath said. "I'll do what I can to help you with the symptoms. As for the cause, I know a guy who's much better qualified to handle a demon like this one than I am. And you won't find anyone more discreet."

"Thank you," DeAndre said, relief all over his face and all through his voice.

"Don't thank me yet," Heath said with a wicked smile. "You haven't heard what I'm charging you for this."

2

DeAndre didn't even try to haggle. Heath was a little disappointed, to tell the truth. But then he saw what DeAndre was driving, and realized he could probably have charged ten times as much as he did.

Sitting at the curb just outside of Powell's was a huge Lexus. An LX 450, black, gleaming in the early afternoon sunlight, and as loaded as they came. The thing looked big enough that it should have had an access ladder instead of a passenger-side door.

It chirped when Andre pointed at it, even though he didn't have a fob in his hands that Heath could see. And he either already unlocked the doors, or he didn't bother keeping them locked.

Heath was curious as to which it was. Curious enough to feel the desire to know burning a little in his stomach. But he was resolved not to ask.

Colin, however, seemed to have no hesitation.

"Do you keep it unlocked?"

"Usually," DeAndre said with a grimace. "Right now, though, I'm lucky it's not ticketed."

All three of them got in, DeAndre in the driver's seat, Heath riding shotgun, and Colin in the backseat, his two sacks of books on the floor behind DeAndre.

Heath was a little surprised that Colin was tagging along, but DeAndre didn't seem to mind.

The interior was all leather, and it still smelled like a new car. Even though Heath could see that the odometer had more than thirty thousand miles on it.

"Love my baby," DeAndre said, caressing the steering wheel. "Guys tried to talk me into the Mercedes or the Beemer, but no. Wanted one of these since I was a kid." DeAndre looked over at Heath. "You know, Biggie drove one just like this. Older model though."

"Who?" Heath asked, adjusting his seat belt.

DeAndre looked scandalized.

"Yeah," Colin said from the back seat. "Heath knows modern music like priests know the best places to get laid."

DeAndre laughed, while Colin continued.

"Heath, Biggie Smalls, also known as the Notorious B.I.G., also known as Big Poppa, was a very skilled and popular rapper in the 90s. He was shot to death."

With that last sentence, DeAndre kissed the first two fingertips of his right hand, and held them skyward in tribute to his fallen hero.

"Okay," Heath said with a shrug.

DeAndre shook his head, started the car with the push of a button, and pulled them into traffic.

Traffic treated DeAndre's car like it was any other car. And since it was only just about one in the afternoon, the last vestiges of lunchtime traffic were still slowing the streets of downtown Portland.

This was strange.

Heath's own car could slip through traffic like a katana through gelatin. Though maybe that comparison was more apt for the way Nariko sliced through traffic on her sleek silver motorcycle.

Both vehicles, enchanted to make sure that traffic treated them right, and that cops and accidents stayed far away.

Colin didn't have any permanent enchantments on his own

Saturn sedan, but Colin must have had some on himself that made up the difference, because Colin rarely had the kind of trouble with traffic that a lot of people had these days.

"Lots of traffic today," Heath said, one eyebrow high.

"First clue that things were going wrong," DeAndre said through a grimace. "I've even gotten a speeding ticket. And they searched my ride like they thought I was still slinging cane."

Heath hated to defend the police, but given DeAndre's old occupation, he figured DeAndre might still give off that vibe to those who looked for it.

Still, Heath kept that observation to himself, rather than kick a man who was already down.

"Where are we going?" DeAndre said.

"Lake Oswego," Heath answered, naming the Portland suburb south along the Willamette River, where the help Heath had in mind could be found.

"Just give me directions as we go," DeAndre said. He hesitated, then added, "The GPS was the second clue."

It was true that downtown Portland remembered to mix in some tall buildings among all the trees and grass. It was also true that what Portland considered a tall building was like comparing a toddler to an NBA center, compared to what Heath had known during his teenage years in Manhattan.

Heath had to admit, though, that the longer he lived out here, the more he liked it. Helped keep Portland's small town vibe.

Traffic, though, was one of the signs of Portland's growth. The streets and freeways were not designed to handle as many people as lived and worked in the greater Portland area these days.

DeAndre kept his car under the speed limit, and made sure to signal more than well enough in advance for any lane changes or turns. If Heath hadn't known better, he might have thought DeAndre was driving like he was on his way to a hit.

"So," DeAndre said as they drove. "Hear you were down the coast recently." His eyes flicked to Heath and back to the road. "California, I hear?"

"Yep," Heath said, not adding any details.

"Is it true you saw a Bigfoot down there?"

"Nope," Heath said, closing his eyes and leaning back against the seat. "Just a small group of werewolves, messing with the locals."

First werewolves Heath had ever heard of forming a pack. For that matter, first werewolves Heath ever heard of that acted like anything other than whirlwinds of murder and destruction.

But he didn't feel enough like sharing to tell DeAndre that, and he'd already told Colin.

"Find anything interesting down there?"

Heath let the question lay long enough that Colin cleared his throat.

Apparently, Colin was interested in seeing Heath make friends with DeAndre, even if Heath wasn't.

"It was a trip I promised one of my spirits. A good helper."

True, in the sense that Heath's car, the *Parakeet*, had a strong spirit of its own. It was the *Parakeet* he'd promised the drive.

Silence reigned for a few long minutes, with nothing more than the sound of traffic and Colin's drumming fingers to break the tension.

"Did collect some good redwood and sequoia bark, needles and twigs though."

"Yeah?" DeAndre said. "What are they good for?"

First question of any conjure worker, Heath mused. What can I use it for?

"Don't know yet," Heath said. "Figure I'll experiment with them. Picked up a few other things for much the same reason."

"Cool," DeAndre said. "Cool."

Another minute or so of silence. Traffic had thinned now, as they got farther from downtown. They were on a highway now that ran down near the Willamette. They'd be in Lake Oswego soon.

DeAndre glanced over at Heath, then back at the road.

"I figured out for myself some of the uses of this mushroom I found growing over in the Hollywood District."

"Yeah?" Colin said with interest, probably thinking of a very different kind of mushroom.

"Yes," DeAndre continued, when he saw Heath look over with some curiosity. "Black, with red spots. Dry them out, but don't crumble them. Let them sit for two days, then steep them in a verbena tea. Drink the tea, but don't eat the mushrooms. Pray over them the words from first Simon, twenty-two-twenty-three. If anyone's trying to hex you or lay a trick on you, you'll see their image in your head."

First book of Simon, chapter twenty-two, verse twenty-three. Heath knew that one. *The man who wants to kill you is trying to kill me too. You will be safe with me.*

"Not bad," Heath said with a slow nod.

DeAndre flashed a bright smile to hear a compliment from Heath.

"How the fuck did you figure that out?" Colin asked.

"Got to talk to the plants," Heath and DeAndre said at the same time.

Then Heath shared a laugh with DeAndre for the first time.

Heath had to admit, he was feeling relaxed and a little more positive about helping this man as he gave the final directions to where they were going.

———

DeAndre actually pulled into the parking lot and found a spot for that huge Lexus of his — even turned off the engine — before he turned and asked the question Heath had been waiting for.

"Is this a joke?"

The question was inevitable. Heath had just given DeAndre directions to a cemetery. And not a new one. This cemetery was one of the oldest in the area, with graves going back all the way to the Oregon Trail days.

Looked beautiful, too. Rolling hills, and plenty of majestic Douglas firs.

"Nope," Heath said, and popped off his seatbelt. He turned to get out of the car, but Colin cleared his throat again.

Heath turned a dirty look back over his shoulder, but Colin had this be-good expression on his face. Like he was going to tell Nariko on Heath, if Heath managed to end up making anything less than a friend on this little venture.

Obviously Colin had missed a vital element in Nariko's personality. She suffered fools and bullshit even less than Heath did.

If DeAndre had gone to Nariko for help, she would have laughed in his face and told him to twist in the wind.

She wouldn't have lost a moment's sleep over it.

But then, Nariko didn't make her living selling spells. And she hadn't been through what Heath had gone through. Heath knew Nariko had her own problems with a mother that was ... worse than anything Heath could have imagined. Heck, he suspected she was out at Mount Hood to build up her power, largely because of her mother.

Not easy, being the daughter of a dragon.

But Heath's uncle was more than a little like the way this Papa Dusk sounded. And Heath, well, if his life had been different — if he hadn't had his grandmother's influence, and some help from Papa Legba — Heath might have ended up walking down some of the same paths DeAndre had trod.

Heath didn't relish looking into this dark mirror though.

Still. Maybe DeAndre deserved a little more explanation.

Heath settled back into the leather of the front passenger seat.

"Yes," Heath said, "this is a cemetery. But it's not a joke. And before you ask, we're not here for the graves, and we're not here for the dead, and we're not here for the gravediggers."

"All right," DeAndre said with a frown after Heath eliminated the three main reasons a conjure man might look for help in a graveyard. "Then who are we here for?"

"You remember my friend Tony?"

DeAndre shook his head.

"He was there for that big showdown at Gripper I had with Drake a few weeks back. The monk."

"Oh, yeah," DeAndre said slowly. "Rough and tumble type? Looks kind of like a mob enforcer, dresses all in black that's too heavy for the weather, little rim of black hair around a big bald spot. Right?"

"Tonsured," Colin said. "They call it tonsured when they wear their hair like that deliberately."

"They can call it anything they like," DeAndre said. "It's a terrible look." He ran his hand across his shiny pate. "Much better to shave it down smooth."

"Anyway," Heath said, "Tony's a member of the Protective Order of Saint Benedict. And I've already seen him kick one demon's ass, without so much as a warm-up. If anyone's up to Rochonzon, I'd say he is."

"And he'll do it?" DeAndre raised an eyebrow. "He gonna set me back another five figure fee?"

"Up to him," Heath said. "I'm earning some of my fee just providing the introduction. Without me, you wouldn't even *find* Tony, much less get him to help."

Only about half true, that statement. DeAndre *might* have been able to find the Protective Order of Saint Benedict. If he thought to look for them. God knew DeAndre's need was strong enough, and that was key. But he wouldn't have known where to look.

As for Tony's help, well, Tony was the kind of monk who gave Catholics a good name. No way he'd turn down a man in need.

Of course, he wouldn't likely say no to a donation either.

And yet, Colin let Heath's statement go without clearing his throat or throwing Heath a baleful glance. Maybe he wasn't as forgiving of DeAndre as Heath had started to think.

"All right," DeAndre said. "I trust you. It's just, the way this looked."

"Come on," Heath said. "I did take your money, didn't I?"

"In advance," DeAndre said.

Heath chuckled as he got out of the car. Chose not to point out that if things didn't go well, DeAndre wouldn't be able to pay afterwards.

But then, Heath was sure DeAndre knew that.

Early afternoon here in Lake Oswego, with the clear sky a pale blue up above, and the sun almost lemon yellow, and not too bright or hot. The breeze smelled like firs and an odd mix of flowers. Cars along the nearby road frequent enough for their engines to blend into a background buzz.

Heath led Colin and DeAndre across the tarmac of the parking lot, then away from the funeral parlor and deep into the cemetery.

DeAndre had just started throwing Heath quizzical looks when Heath led them away from the graves, and toward the copses of Douglas firs at the back of the property.

"Are you sure about this?" DeAndre asked. "Maybe we should—"

"Shhh," Heath said, raising one finger to his lips for emphasis. "You've got a lot going on in your head right now. I get that. Makes you prime fodder for their main line of defense. So I want you to take a deep breath, and listen with your thoughts."

DeAndre took that deep breath, and as big as the man was, he seemed have a nigh-infinite capacity for air.

But as he let that slow breath out he started laughing. Softly, out of respect for the dead, but still a laugh.

"Son of a bitch," DeAndre whispered. "They put an *ignore-me* charm on their building?"

"Not quite," Heath said. The monks' magic didn't work the way an *ignore-me* charm would work, but it was close enough. "More like an *is-this-important?* charm."

"Close to it, at least," DeAndre said. Then he closed his eyes and mumbled something. Likely a quick prayer.

DeAndre opened his eyes.

"Ta-da," Heath said, sweeping one hand out wide.

DeAndre could now see what Heath was leading him to.

Tucked behind those Douglas firs was a building entirely too big to just hide in plain sight.

It was two stories tall — three if you included the bell tower — and it was made of smooth, fitted stone, with a minimum of mortar. As though the monks had brought their old world construction methods with them here to the new world.

The windows were narrow and had wooden shutters, and the front door a few dozen paces ahead of them looked heavy enough to make a tank consider finding an easier point of entrance.

The door was made from planks of a rough, dark wood, and bound twice in heavy iron bands. No knob or latch that Heath could see, though the door did have a miniature version of itself set about head height, that could open inward.

Heath thumped a *shave and a haircut* pattern on the door, and turned a smile to DeAndre and Colin. Colin looked eager. DeAndre looked uncertain. Maybe still feeling some effects from the prayers — or whatever the monks called their magic — that kept most potential interlopers away.

A moment later the mini, viewing door opened up.

And the face on the other side was female.

That was unexpected. So far as Heath knew, this was purely a monastic order, and only admitted monks, not nuns.

Then again, this woman wore her short blonde hair tonsured, not tucked under a wimple.

Huh.

She had the kind of fresh-faced look that made Heath think she might not be old enough to drink. But then he saw her eyes. Smoke gray, and those eyes had seen more life than her years indicated.

"Yes," she said, in the kind of perfect deadpan that could probably make a traveling salesman's balls tuck themselves back up into his body.

Certainly Colin hissed in a breath as though maybe thinking this was a bad idea.

"Hi," Heath said with a big smile. "I'm a friend of Brother Anthony's. Heath Cyr. I'm here with his friend Colin as well, and a man who needs his help."

The woman stared at Heath for a moment, as though trying to decide if Heath was telling the truth.

Odd.

"I'm sorry," Heath said. "Not sure where my manners are. What's your name?"

Nothing.

She started to close the mini-door.

"Hold on now," Heath said, one hand coming up to stop that mini-door from closing. "I'm telling you the truth. If you don't believe me, ask Brother Anthony. Or if you don't believe him, ask Brother Theodopolis."

At the mention of the head of at least the local chapter of her order, the female monk frowned.

"I mean it," Heath said. "I'm the one who brought the *Black Book of Saint Cyprian* here a couple of months back."

At the mention of that especially evil grimoire the woman monk — lady monk? Female monk? Heath couldn't decide what the proper term would be, so he just decided to call her a monk from here on out — crossed herself, and nodded.

"One moment," she said, in that same deadpan voice.

Heath had to let her close the little door though. Otherwise, he was pretty sure Tony would never know Heath had arrived.

"You're sure these people will help?" DeAndre muttered.

"Trust me," Heath said, feeling a little less confident than he had before. "I know they won't let us down."

And if they did, they might find that Heath Cyr was not going to be so staunch an ally as he had been for them so far.

Nearby western meadowlarks were singing in the Douglas firs. Cars went past in the background, as though adding bass to the bird songs.

And here, in the step of this archaic stone building, Heath was starting to feel like a fool.

Colin was humming to himself. No doubt one of his heavy metal songs.

DeAndre straightened his shoulders and cuffs a good dozen times. As though standing there might wrinkle his suit. Somehow.

Heath tried to maintain himself as the model of patience while the three of them waited for someone — anyone at this point — to open that front door and admit them into the outer sanctum of the Protective Order of Saint Benedict.

"At least it's not raining," Heath muttered to himself. Had it been even a week deeper into September, it might have been.

Heath had just started tapping the toe of his boat shoes when the front door of the stone monastery opened up, at last.

Standing there was Tony, dressed as Heath had always seen him, in black wool from collar to his black loafers.

But Tony's mouth spread wide in a big smile.

"Heath!" he said, and swept Heath up in a bear hug. "Too long since I've seen you. What's it been, a week?"

"Eight days," Heath said. "That was when we went for pizza at that little place you knew."

"Fantastic pizza," Colin said, sounding as though he wished they were there right now.

And he might have. None of them had eaten all that much today — well, Heath and Colin hadn't, but Heath couldn't be sure about DeAndre. Certainly Heath hadn't had more than a chocolate muffin, and his quick metabolism had long since burned through that.

"Colin!" Tony said, stepping past DeAndre to sweep the skinny man with the long blond hair up into a tight embrace. "Good to see you as always."

Colin was laughing. He always laughed when Tony picked him up. Heath figured that was at least half the reason Tony did it.

Finally Tony turned to DeAndre.

And Tony's voice got formal.

"DeAndre McDaniels, I believe?" Tony said, holding out one hand.

"That's right," DeAndre said, shaking Tony's offered hand. "And I believe Heath said you're Brother Anthony?"

"Only formally," Tony said as the handshake ended on its own time. "If you're here with Heath, you can call me Tony."

Tony glanced over at Heath, then Tony's brown eyes got wide as if seeking confirmation.

"Yep," Heath confirmed. "DeAndre here is the man with a problem and the reason we had to bug you here at your sanctuary."

"Then you boys better come in."

Tony led the way inside. And the inside of the building looked as handcrafted as the outside.

The floor and walls were the same fitted stone, and inside they were fitted tightly enough that they didn't need even a little mortar to hold them together.

Even in the summertime warmth, the stone hall was cool. And as they moved down the hall, the torches they passed in occasional sconces lit when they neared, and went out again as they passed.

They walked as though in a gentle bubble of light, surrounded by darkness.

The air in here smelled of baked bread, and frankincense.

Down the hall they went, but not to Tony's room. Instead, Tony led them past the monks' personal rooms, into a small office.

And this office was small. Ceiling not much more than seven feet up, and the room itself was barely big enough for a desk and stool along one wall, a three-drawer filing cabinet under a bookshelf on the second, and wooden, high-backed bench along the third.

If Heath was feeling cramped in here, he could only imagine how DeAndre had to be feeling. But the big man didn't look any more uncomfortable here than he had while waiting outside.

Still, small as the office was, it was comfortable enough. Everything in the room looked to have been lovingly made by hand from a blonde hardwood, sanded smooth held together by wooden pegs, rather than nails.

On the desk were scrolls of parchment, along with an inkwell, actual freaking quills, and an ink blotter. Above the desk, a small painting of Saint Benedict, one hand raised in benediction.

Colin stared longingly at the single shelf of books. They were bound in leather, and might have been as handmade as everything else in the room seemed to be.

This was only the second time Heath had been inside the monastery, and last time Heath had been carrying *The Black Book of*

Saint Cyprian, a cursed relic that was as alive as it was evil. He hadn't been in a position to appreciate the feel of the air in here.

The place actually felt holy. In that way churches and cathedrals were always supposed to feel, but so rarely did.

At least, the ones that Heath had been to.

The air itself in here seemed to carry a sense of peace, welcome and safety.

Tony sat on his stool. Colin sank down cross-legged on the floor under the shelf of books, as though he hoped to absorb something from them by osmosis.

That left the bench for DeAndre and Heath. Heath gestured for DeAndre, and was pleasantly surprised that DeAndre sat to one side, leaving room for Heath.

Heath had half-expected the cramped conditions to make DeAndre take as much room on the bench as he could, just to be more comfortable.

Once all four were seated, Tony said, "Magdalene said you had a problem, but she didn't give me any details."

"I'm sorry," DeAndre said, and to his credit, he did look apologetic. Had one hand over his heart and one extended forward as though apologizing. "That woman was a *monk*, not a nun?"

"Well," Tony said, one eyebrow raised and his lips scowling just a little, "technically she's in training to become a monk. She's not one yet. But she will be a monk, yes, not a nun. She will be Brother Magdalene, not Sister Magdalene. The Protective Order of Saint Benedict does not have a sister order of nuns. However, our charter says nothing about admitting only men."

Tony grinned. "Most of the orders don't, to be honest. Because it's just been *pro forma* that only men apply to them and are admitted. We're ... a little unusual in that we encourage membership from women. So long as they've had the kind of experiences we're looking for in the order."

"Contact with the supernatural?" DeAndre asked.

"Essentially," Tony said. "The details don't matter at the moment."

"I do believe that woman has seen some *shit*," DeAndre said.

"Tell me about the problem," Tony said, plainly changing the subject. "I can see that a black cloud hangs over you, DeAndre. Care to tell me why that is?"

DeAndre looked at Heath.

"Brother Tony," Heath said, "would you extend to DeAndre the privacy of the confessional for this? He needs to tell you the whole story if you're going to help him, but, well, there are good reasons he's hesitant to just come out and talk."

Tony's eyes widened. No doubt his mind went straight to the right conclusion. After all, there was no statute of limitations on murder.

"Are you Catholic?" Tony asked DeAndre.

"Presbyterian," DeAndre answered.

"Then I'm not going to offer you confession, unless you ask for it. However," Tony said, raising one hand before DeAndre could speak. "Don't ask for the confessional unless you truly wish to confess and repent your sins. This is not a requirement for my help."

DeAndre looked helplessly at Heath.

Heath started to ask the question, but Tony answered before he could.

"What I'm saying is that I will treat anything you tell me in this room with the same sanctity as I would anything told to me in confession. This is unusual, but the nature of my order's work is such that I may do this."

DeAndre frowned. "Forgive me, but I have to ask. Don't you have to be a priest to offer confession?"

"Yes," Tony said, then smiled. "*Oh.* Technically, yes, I am Father Antonio, but please do not call me that here. You see, all members of this order are referred to as brothers, whether they have taken the vows of priesthood or not. Just one of the ways in which we are unusual."

Then Tony frowned. "And it occurs to me I must amend my statement, for clarity. Right now I do not know what you will tell me, nor what resources will be necessary to bring forth to deal with the problems you face. It may be that more members of my order will be needed, and if so, I will ask you to share this information with them as well, with the understanding that your information will go no further. Is this agreeable to you?"

DeAndre glanced at Heath, who nodded. "You can trust their discretion."

"In for a drop," DeAndre muttered, then louder said, "I can agree to that."

Apparently DeAndre had now run out of excuses to stall, because he told his story. Heath was impressed that Colin managed to hear the whole thing — he'd missed part of it in the coffee shop when he'd gone to fetch coffee — without making any sounds louder than a gasp.

For his part, Brother Tony took the whole story with only sympathy and concern.

Except for the parts mentioning the demon. Those seemed to ignite a blaze behind Tony's brown eyes.

"Rochonzon," Tony said, when DeAndre was finished. "The demon said to guard the abyss. Or, according to some, the demon said to be the mouth of the abyss. The container for the whole of the demons that dwell within."

Tony shook his head. "This Papa Dusk didn't go small, did he?"

"Can you help me?" DeAndre asked.

"I think so," Tony said with a sigh. "I'm certainly willing to try. You must understand though. This is not a case where a demon has lured you into corruption, or tricked you. This Papa Dusk might have misled you a bit, or misrepresented aspects of what you were doing, but for the most part you went into it with your eyes open. You knew you were committing murder. You knew this murder was for purposes of sacrifice to a demon. And you planned on materially benefiting from this sacrifice."

Tony leaned forward on his stool.

"Do you understand what I'm saying? You're not a victim in this. You are an evildoer, who is receiving the comeuppances of his evil deeds. To many, this would be a case of justice."

"But not to you?"

Was that hope Heath heard in DeAndre's voice.

"No," Tony said with an emphatic shake of his head. "It is not my place to judge you or your actions. That is a role reserved for God Himself. I am only a man. And as a man I can look on another man who is suffering, and perhaps ease his suffering while inhibiting the work of a demon in this world."

DeAndre sighed and leaned back against the bench.

"However," Tony said, and DeAndre leaned forward again. "I am also a priest. And as a priest, I can tell you that you have committed murder and idolatry. Both of these are major sins, and you will have to look to your sins and your own conscious, and deal with them as you will."

"I ... see," DeAndre said.

"But if I am going to do battle with a demon on your behalf, then I need to know what weapons it will bring to bear." Tony squared his shoulders and faced DeAndre head on. "I need to know if you truly repent what you've done. Not that you are sorry that the bill has come due, but that you are sorry to have murdered this man, sorry to have offered him up to a demon."

DeAndre, to his credit, took a moment to think before speaking.

"I regretted the demon part as soon as I did it." He shook his head. "I caught a brief vision of the thing when it showed up to claim its sacrifice, and I knew right then that this demon was evil on a whole order of magnitude beyond anything I could ever be. Maybe even beyond anything Papa Dusk could ever be."

"And the murder?"

DeAndre blew out a long, slow breath. Shook his head.

"I regret offering that guard up to the demon. That I truly do. What I saw when the demon showed up. What I felt. No one should have to suffer under that thing. But the murder itself?" DeAndre shook his head. "That guard was an evil mother fucker, and he deserved to have his throat slit by the inmates he abused."

"You going to do that Archangel Michael thing?" Colin asked. "Test the truth of his words that way?"

"Don't need to," Tony said. "I can tell you're telling me the absolute truth, DeAndre. And I appreciate that."

Tony sighed. "I wish you repented the whole thing though. Holding on to your hatred of that guard is going to make our work harder."

"Anything I can do to help?" Heath asked.

"Undoubtedly," Tony said with a smile. "But before I can take another step, I must speak with the head of my order. If you gentlemen would be so kind as to wait here for me."

And Brother Tony swept out of the room, leaving the three of them alone.

THE SMALL OFFICE SOMEHOW FELT EVEN SMALLER WITHOUT BROTHER Tony. The monk had only been out of the office a handful of seconds, and already the bench Heath sat on with DeAndre felt as though it had shrunk. And Colin sitting there, cross-legged on the stone floor, felt close enough that Heath might accidentally kick him.

Heath was tempted to move over the Tony's vacated stool. Maybe to redress the imbalance of the monk's absence. But Colin broke the moment by speaking.

"Think he'd mind if I did some reading while we wait?"

Maybe it was the simplicity of Colin being Colin, but that sense of compression in the room lifted. Heath smiled at the lustful gaze Colin had turned upon that bookshelf above him.

"If you thought he'd okay it," Heath said, "you'd've asked before he stepped out."

DeAndre laughed. "You really will read anything, won't you?"

"Yep," Colin said. "And you'd be surprised at some of the deep secrets of reality I've learned from the least likely places."

DeAndre shook his head. "Reality itself has a lot more to teach you than books ever will. Take a walk in Forest Park sometime. Try listening to what the animals and plants have to say. You might just be surprised how much there is to learn."

That felt uncomfortably close to something Heath himself might have said. And Colin caught that point. Turned a raised eyebrow on Heath.

Heath shrugged. "We're both root workers. You have to assume we'll have a little bit in common."

"Speaking of," DeAndre said, turning to face Heath. "Maybe when all this is over, you and I should sit down and have a real talk."

"At Gripper?" Colin asked.

"I was thinking someplace more private. Doing anything at Gripper is a statement." DeAndre moved his hands out and back, like he thought about a shrug and changed his mind. "I'm interested in the conversation we could have, not the statement it might make."

Heath wasn't sure how he wanted to answer that one. DeAndre was still the man who had been more interested in threatening Heath than in talking shop with him. Having to come to Heath for help didn't change that. For all Heath knew, the moment this crisis was over, DeAndre would go back to being a raging dick.

Then again, that might only be a self-fulfilling prophecy. If Heath treated DeAndre like a dick...

"I don't know," Heath said, lips pulled wide and flat. "Let's talk about that when we resolve with your problem."

"True," DeAndre said. "If I'm a dead man, I can't..."

"What?" Heath asked when DeAndre didn't finish his sentence. Something about the way the big man just broke off what he was saying gave Heath a cold feeling trickling down his back.

"What if..." DeAndre said, and he grimaced as though the very thought occurring to him right then tasted bad enough he would rather vomit it up than speak it.

But his words came out all the same.

"What if Papa Dusk made some deal with this Rochonzon about what happens after I die?"

"You mean like a zombie?" Colin asked, looking over at Heath.

"No," Heath said, slowly. "Zombies wouldn't be a Rochonzon thing. I mean, I don't know much about demons of that sort, but I know a thing or two about zombies, and if Papa Dusk wasn't working with the Ghedes and Barons, he doesn't have the power to make zombies."

"Not real zombies then," Colin said, standing up now, "but whatever that equivalent is."

"Whatever those plans are," DeAndre said — and Heath could see actual fear in the man's eyes now — "I need to scrap them."

"One thing at a time," Heath said, voice brimming with more confidence than he felt. "Tony'll get the demon off your back. Then we can—"

Heath's phone rang, the opening notes of "Dans Kalinda Ba Boom" by Dr. John.

"I have to take this," Heath said, answering and stepping out into the narrow stone hallway before anyone could stop him. This was a phone call he didn't expect until later in the evening.

"Nariko," Heath said, answering the phone. "What's wrong?"

"Where is my daughter, Mr. Cyr?"

Heath would have known that sharp, condescending tone anywhere.

"Mrs. Tachibana."

This wasn't good. Nariko's mother had never called him before. And she'd certainly never magically spoofed her daughter's phone number, to make sure Heath answered.

To be honest, Heath hadn't even known she could do that. It was a more flagrant use of power than Heath was accustomed to seeing from Nariko's mother.

But that had to be how she called. If Mrs. Tachibana had been holding Nariko's cell phone...

"My daughter," she said. "Where is she?"

"Well, last I heard from Michiko, she was thinking of doing some graduate work down in Corvallis, and as for your youngest—"

"Those two have more than enough sense to stay away from a man as undesirable as you are, Mr. Cyr. I speak of my daughter Nariko, as you know I do. And if you do not tell me, I shall become very cross with you, Mr. Cyr. I believe my daughter has given you some idea of what that means?"

Nariko had never mentioned the specifics of what her mother could or could not do. Then again, Nariko had seemed quite certain that her mother had all too few limitations.

Mrs. Tachibana was, after all, a mountain dragon, and quite old.

"Look," Heath said through a sigh. "If you're going to go saying nasty things to me like that, you're not exactly giving me incentive to play nice. Now are you?"

"I am not interested in playing nice. I am interested in—"

"Finding your daughter." Heath sighed again. "Hate to tell you, but I don't know where she is. You might have noticed that I sounded a little worried when I picked up the phone."

Tricky thing, deceiving a dragon. Technically Heath's words had been true. He didn't know *exactly* where Nariko was. He knew only a general area where he *expected* her to be. Add that *general* truth to the *specific* truth that he had sounded worried when he thought Nariko was calling early, and the whole thing probably tasted as true as anything Heath was likely to say to her.

There was a reason even DeAndre respected Heath's trickiness.

"Hmmm," she said, which was as close as she ever came to admitting Heath was right about anything.

"Besides," Heath added. "Can't say I'd feel too inclined to tell you, if I did know. Your daughter's an adult, you know. If Nariko wanted you to know where she was, she'd tell you."

Heath spotted a torch flaring to life down the hall. Heard the sound of approaching leather soles on stone.

"Now if you'll excuse me," Heath said, "I have to see about saving a man's soul."

As Tony approached, Heath had the great satisfaction of hanging up on Nariko's mother.

"Everything all right?" Tony asked as Heath put his phone away.

"I should be asking you that," Heath said.

But Tony frowned, his eyes still on the pocket where Heath had stashed his phone.

"Outside cell phones shouldn't work here," Tony said. "Disturbs the peace. Even our own phones only work in designated rooms."

"Nariko's mom's looking for her."

Tony's frown expanded to include a wrinkle between his eyebrows. "I know Nariko's what you call a 'heavy hitter,' but..."

Heath clapped a hand on Tony's shoulder. He looked the into the monk's brown eyes and said, "Nariko's mother is ... complicated. And a conversation for another time."

"Right," Tony said, in a tone that clearly sounded like a rain check. "The problem in front of us first."

"Words to live by," Heath said with a smile he didn't quite feel.

And as Tony led the way back into his office, Heath offered up a small prayer to keep Nariko safe while she did ... whatever it was she was doing out there.

3

―――――

Tony didn't just lead Heath, Colin and DeAndre into a special room. He led them down a stone flight of stairs past the basement, past the sub-basement, all the way to what had to be a sub-sub-basement.

This was deeper underground than Heath generally liked to be, and he had a little trouble at first stopping himself from thinking about exactly how much weight of stone and earth was above him, and exactly how flat it could all squish him if it all came tumbling down right now.

Thinking about it made the back of Heath's neck itch, and made his skull feel just oh-so-vulnerable.

It was that thought that made Heath pause on the steps. When he did, he could just barely make out the faint strains of Ghede Brav's laughter.

Odd, that hearing the laughter of a Lwa, especially one of the Ghedes, who were all aspects of death, would make Heath feel better. But it did. Almost made him laugh.

After all, if everything collapsed on his head right now, it would be a quick death, and he'd already be buried. Maman Brigitte might have trouble collecting his bones though. They'd be powdered.

That laugh also reminded Heath that he still had Ghede Brav's flask, and had to figure out just how he was going to return it before the Lwa came looking for it.

But that was a problem for later. Right this moment, Heath needed his thoughts here with him. Right exactly where he was, on what exactly he was doing.

Air was cool down here, but not moist. Dry. That was odd. Heath had been expecting the air to moisten a little as they came down. Or at least stay as moist as it usually was here around Portland.

And the smell was dry too. More like all there was to smell down here was the stone itself.

At least, until Tony led them into the ritual chamber.

Heath had heard about ritual chambers. He'd never had anything like one himself, of course. The kind of root work and conjure magic he did was intended to be done anywhere, often on the spur of the moment.

Anything that required a special "chamber" was just too damned much trouble.

Still, Heath knew a ritual chamber when he saw one.

Forty feet long, easy, and maybe thirty across. The ceiling height was only about ten feet, and it was stone as solid as any he'd seen so far. Down here it was all mortared together, in addition to the tight fit the stone masons had used.

There was an altar at one end, with a crucifix above it — carved from a dark wood Heath didn't recognize — and generally looking a lot like the kind of altar he expected catholic priests to use. White cloth, trimmed in gold. An incense censer. Candles (which had sprung to light when Tony entered, and right now provided the only light in the room). A bible. A bottle of communion wine with a gold chalice beside it. A tray of rye bread, no doubt waiting to be blessed for use in the sacrament. Jars of holy water.

All those things were to be expected. Though the sight and smell of a loaf of fresh rye bread set Heath's stomach to growling. That muffin had been hours ago now...

What Heath did not expect on the altar was the black mirror, a gleaming disc of obsidian, perhaps two feet in diameter, resting on a purple cloth. Nor the collection of what were obviously grimoires and just as obviously hundreds of years old.

Heath could practically *hear* Colin start salivating at the sight of those books. Of course, he wouldn't want to use their magic. For magic, Colin only liked the modern stuff. But as he'd said, he'd read anything. No matter how archaic.

The two knives were also a surprise, one black-handled and one white-handled. Both had letters in some foreign language written on the sides. As did what was obviously a wand: a stick of rowan about two feet long, sanded and polished, with the letters burnt in. Other strange things included a sealed vase, with more writing on it, a series of candles in different colors, none of which were lit, and, oh yes, the huge freaking sword hanging on pegs beside the altar.

Still, the most obvious sign that this was a ritual chamber? The great big freaking hexagram in a circle in the center of the room. It was about ten feet across, and set into the stone in white marble. Hebrew letters had also been inset into the stone, using more white marble.

Nearby was another symbol, inscribed in the floor. A triangle, inset in black marble, maybe five feet across, with more Hebrew.

"Karcist," Colin teased Tony, using the word that some of the Western Ceremonialists used. Especially ones that favored summoning demons.

"Hey," Tony said with a smile, "remember, a lot of those original grimoires were actually written by monks and priests."

"No shit?" DeAndre said. "I thought they were supposed to be written by ancient Greeks or 'mad Arabs' or something."

"Propaganda," Tony said. Then shook his head. "We're not down here for that kind of magic though."

"You mean we're *not* summoning a demon?" Heath asked, edging in around DeAndre and trying to decide whether he could actually do any good during whatever Tony had in mind. And what he could be doing if Tony didn't need him.

He had an idea or two...

"Oh, we are," Tony said with a confident smile. "But you must understand that different approaches require different forms of authority and yield different results. If we summoned Rochonzon in a formal ritual magic way, he'd respond to us in a very different way than if we demand that he come forward, with the full weight of the Church behind me. See the difference?"

DeAndre nodded.

Heath contented himself with a smirk and a slight nod. Authority. He knew all about it. No spirit respected you unless you had something going for you. Heath had plenty of authority on his own, but he couldn't wait to see — from a purely professional standpoint — exactly what Brother Tony looked like when he was operating with the "full weight of the Church" behind him.

"Tony," Colin said, as Tony knelt and pulled a chest out from under the altar. It was a big, heavy thing of smooth blonde hardwood, with iron bands and clasps that locked in three places.

Tony didn't use a key. The locks just opened for him when he needed them to. Just another example of authority, as long as Heath was thinking about it.

"Tony," Colin tried again as Tony pulled out a long, pure white linen stole and draped it over his shoulders. A sharp contrast with the monk's black clothes.

Tony kissed the ends. Muttered a quick prayer that Heath thought warmed the room just a hair.

Only then did Tony open his eyes and say, "Yes, Colin?"

Was it Heath's imagination, or did Tony *actually* sound more priestly when he said that?

Colin ducked his head for a moment.

"Um, look. DeAndre, he's the guy you're trying to save. And Heath, he may not be a Catholic anymore, really, but he's still at least a Christian. But me, I'm just about as agnostic as they come."

"I thought you were one of those chaos magic types," Tony said with a frown.

Oh, no.

Heath tried to get Tony's attention, but it was too late. The monk kept talking, clearly not knowing what he was stepping into.

"Free to work with any set of beliefs, or something like that."

Colin's eyes narrowed in the kind of anger rarely seen in a guy so laid back. Even DeAndre gave a step before the sight, though it was probably surprise more than fear or respect.

"Chaos magic?" Colin shook his head like he didn't believe what he'd just heard. Already his face was passing red on its way to purple. *"Chaos magic?"*

Colin shook his head harder, so hard his long blonde hair whipped about him.

"You aren't then?" Tony ventured, but it was too late.

The rant was already underway.

"Those dilettantes! Those *idiots!* They think because they can find a little piece of magic in a system that they can just dance in and dance out again any time they like? And there are no consequences?"

"Whoa," Heath said, hands coming up as he stepped over to intervene.

"'Oh, we're just like Bruce Lee. The Jeet Kun Do of magic. Tee hee.'"

"Colin..."

"Martial arts is not magic!" Colin yelled. "And Lee *unified!* He didn't just *cherry pick everything out of context!* He learned the context, then adapted his system!"

"Come on, Colin," Heath said, physically grabbing Colin by his shoulders and guiding him back toward the stairs.

"There are *consequences* to what we do! You can't just say, oh, today I'll do the Lesser Banishing Ritual of ... of ... Kermit the Frog. And then tomorrow go back to ignoring Muppets. Spirits are real! They have memories!"

Heath had Colin out of the room and almost to the stairs, but Colin leaned back around him for one more parting shot.

"Gaze into a belief system and the belief system gazes also into you!"

"Go cool off, Colin," Heath said, closing the door in his friend's face.

Heath turned back around, shaking his head.

For a moment, silence reigned. Not a pure silence though. The muffled sound of Colin's ranting could be heard even past that thick door, growing distant. Likely as he ascended the stairs.

"So," DeAndre said at last. "Weird Colin *isn't* a chaos magician then. Got it. Message received."

Heath and Tony started laughing.

"Boy," DeAndre said, smiling now himself. "That is clearly not a question to ask again."

He thought about it a little more, and added, "Well, maybe at Gripper..."

"WELL," HEATH SAID WHEN THEY'D ALL STOPPED LAUGHING. "CLEARLY Colin is not going to do anyone much good for this. What about me though, Tony? As Colin said, I'm just about as far lapsed as a Catholic can get."

"Tosh," Tony said, digging through his crate again. And unless Heath was mistaken, he saw what looked like a lion skin belt in there. He'd already slipped a brass amulet around his neck, engraved with an elaborate sigil of some kind. "Sorry to tell you this, Heath, but once you're baptized, you're in. Besides..."

Tony looked up at Heath. "You had your Catechism, right?"

Heath nodded, "But—"

"No buts. You've confirmed the promises made on your behalf at baptism. You're ours, whether you believe it or not."

Heath chose not to point out that those were the same words he had heard from the Lwa, and he was pretty sure he knew which one he thought had a better claim.

Then again, the Lwa weren't gods. They were mysteries, serving the one true God.

Maybe both were right...

"So, you think I can help then?"

"Yes, you'll serve as acolyte for this. Recite the answers as needed.

I'll give you a cheat sheet." Tony stood, frowning, as though he'd wanted something that he couldn't find in the chest. He shook his head. "DeAndre, stand in the smaller circle."

"Smaller?" He asked, which was the same question Heath might have asked, himself. He hadn't seen a second circle anywhere.

But then Tony pointed, and Heath could make it just make it out in the dim light of the candlesticks. It looked to have been drawn in chalk, not etched in marble. Though the chalk might have been traced over something else. Tough to be sure. The smaller circle was on the other side of the huge hexagram, so it was at least fifteen feet from where Heath stood over by the door.

"Where?" DeAndre asked, craning his neck as he looked.

"My apologies," Tony said. "*Fiat lux.*"

Torches in recessed sconces all around the room lit at the same time, warming the room and giving the chamber a nice, gentle glow.

Heath could now see the second circle clearly. And the chalk was indeed sketched over a slightly darker blue stone that had been used to inscribe it within the stone floor.

DeAndre went where he was bid.

"What about me?" Heath asked.

"You'll join me in the seal of Solomon." And Tony stepped into the middle of the hexagram, which was more than large enough to accommodate them both. Heath adjusted his backpack on his shoulder and joined him.

Tony made a couple of trips back to the altar, including getting Heath the cheat sheet. Tony added incense to the censer and brought back two jars of holy water.

He set these and a few other things down in the hexagram. Tony then set a candle at each corner of the triangle. Two white candles, and one black. White candles were in the corners facing the hexagram and facing the circle DeAndre stood in. The black candle was in the only corner that faced away.

Tony lit those candles from a single match. Heath thought he heard Tony mumbling prayers as he did it.

Tony then placed a single white candle in the center of the

smaller circle, and lit it from its own match. He spared DeAndre a glance.

"Mind you don't knock this over or snuff it out."

"Course not," DeAndre said, but he moved his feet a little farther away.

Tony then returned to the hexagram and lit the censer. The sweet scent of frankincense began to fill the room.

Tony swung the censer, sending out wafts of smoke, while he prayed quietly, in Latin. He carried the censer to the corners of the room, then into the smaller circle, then into the triangle, and at last back into the hexagram. By the time he got there, the lingering smoke had added a faint haze to the air.

"Heath," Tony said, and Heath turned to sand in front of him. "Arms out."

Heath extended his arms to the side.

Tony moved the censer to bathe Heath in frankincense smoke while praying blessings.

Tony set down the censer, then took up the holy water.

He touched Heath with holy water three times on the forehead, while praying more blessings.

Finally, anointing oil came, and Tony applied it to the pulse points in Heath's wrists, behind his ears, and to the center of his forehead. All the while praying more blessings.

Heath had to admit, when Tony was done Heath felt as though he'd been wrapped in a comfortable blanket of ... holy security.

That wasn't quite right, but it was as close as Heath could come at the time.

Tony then quickly repeated the process on himself.

DeAndre had started looking a little nervous, but it was his turn next. Tony came over and stood right in front of the big man.

"DeAndre McDaniels," Tony said in a stentorian voice. "Do you regret sacrificing a human life to the demon Rochonzon?"

"I do," DeAndre said.

"I ask again, *do you regret sacrificing a human life to the demon Rochonzon?*"

"I do," DeAndre said even more firmly.

"I ask one more time. Do you regret sacrificing a human life to the demon Rochonzon?"

"I do."

"Are you willing to forsake all infernal blessings and benefits you have received through this sacrifice?"

DeAndre drew a deep breath before answering, but nodded once. "I am."

"Are you willing to forsake all future infernal benefits and blessings you might receive from this demon?"

"From this demon, or any other demon," DeAndre said, really getting into the spirit of the moment. "From here until the end of time. I want nothing more from demons. I want to be free of them."

"What are you willing to do to be free of them?"

That question, DeAndre wasn't ready for.

"What is required of me?" he asked in an uncertain voice.

"Wrong question," Tony said and gave his head one firm shake. "It is not for me to tell you what you must do. It is not for me to require any action from you. I ask you, what are you willing to do to be freed of demons?"

"Whatever I must," DeAndre said.

"And if that means you must lose all you have?"

"Then I lose all I have." Challenge had entered DeAndre's voice now. As though he were really starting to understand exactly what Tony was saying, and he was ready to do whatever it took.

"Even if it means returning to jail? Even if it leads to your conviction for the murder of that guard?"

DeAndre got quiet. His nostrils flared wide in a deep breath. "I do not regret killing that guard, and I never will. And if being free of this demon means I must pay for that crime, then I will pay that price."

"Good," Tony said. "I do not require this of you. I am only a man, and a man who would inhibit the power of demons in this world. Your sins are your own, and your atonements must be your own."

"Wait," DeAndre said, holding up one hand. "I know one form of atonement I can commit to right now."

"You need not offer this to receive help," Tony said. "And you should not offer it here and now unless you are certain you will follow through. Any promises made here are made in the sight of the Holy Spirit."

"I am certain."

Heath had to admit, DeAndre looked certain. He had a determined look in his eye, his posture was crisp and he held his jaw high.

In that moment, Heath felt a little better about helping DeAndre.

"What atonement to do you have in mind?" Tony asked.

"I am willing to fight to inhibit the power of demons in this world. Once I am freed of Rochonzon, I swear that I will oppose demons and their work wherever I may find them. Even if I do so from inside a prison cell."

Heath couldn't check himself from the soft whistle that made it past his lips. He didn't really want to draw attention to himself, but that was just an unexpected level of commitment from a guy who — at least in Heath's opinion — had always been a little too comfortable working the darker side of the street.

"Excellent," Tony said, and Heath could hear the smile in the monk's voice. "Then you will be welcome among our ranks."

Tony nodded once, and proceeded with the blessings. When he was done, DeAndre had a look of peace in his eyes. Heath couldn't help wondering if he had the same look right now.

"Now," Tony said in a tone that suggested to Heath that Tony had done his share of lecturing. "I'm sure I don't have to tell you not to leave the circle until *I* tell you it's all right. Not Heath, and certainly not anyone or anything else. You stay here. Right?"

DeAndre nodded. "I'll sleep here if I have to."

"You won't," Tony said, "but I appreciate the thought. Now, as for the rest of it. Once we begin, you are not to speak unless I ask you a question. If I do, you are to answer honestly, in a loud, clear voice. Understood?"

"Understood," DeAndre said in a loud, clear voice.

"Good," Tony said with a nod. "Now, the demon will talk to you. Ignoring it is probably too much to ask, but *do not answer it*. Do you understand me? Under no circumstances are you to speak to the demon. If you can, simply look away from it and do your best to ignore it."

"No problem," DeAndre said.

"Oh, this will be a problem," Tony said in a warning voice. "The demon will try to engage you. It may use truth, lies or a combination of the two. But whatever it says, whatever it does, *do not engage it*."

"All right," DeAndre said, but he sounded less certain now.

"The demon has a hold on you, DeAndre. You must understand that. A hold you have given him." And the urgency in Tony's voice made Heath think the monk was trying to *will* the big man to understand. "What we are doing here today is severing that hold. You have come to us of your own free will. You are asking God to free you of this demon. But if you engage the demon, you may reaffirm the connection. Do you understand?"

"I think so," DeAndre said slowly.

"Look at it this way," Heath said. "Say a woman's husband was straying, and she wanted to ditch the son of a bitch. But he wants to fight the divorce. Or maybe he just won't go away. So she comes to you, and you work a little *anywhere-but-here* charm to get rid of him. What happens if she calls him?"

"She wastes all my good work." DeAndre gave Tony a firm nod. "Got it. I'll try not to even look at it."

"Good man," Tony said.

Tony turned and strode back into the center of the seal of Solomon. He muttered a little Latin, and wicks burst into flame at each point of the inscribed hexagram, giving off a pale blue light. The monks must have stashed little pots of lamp oil down there.

He nodded to Heath.

"Now, we are ready to begin."

FOREIGN LANGUAGES WERE NEVER REALLY HEATH'S THING. He understood some French, though he'd been told his own attempts to speak it were atrocious. He had a working knowledge of Kreyol, but he hadn't spoken it conversationally in a very long time.

And honestly, his Grandmother hated for him to speak it. She always thought he should have devoted himself more to French, and his parents agreed.

Heath's mother had even encouraged him, on occasion, to pick up a word or two of Gaelic. Hadn't really taken though. Heath still had trouble believing there could be a language hidden among all those hairball syllables.

So when Tony started rattling off Latin with the speed and assurance of a native speaker, Heath couldn't begin to follow it.

Tony must have been spitting out free-flowing Latin for maybe ten minutes, and by the time he stopped Heath had only really picked out two words.

Deus, which he knew meant God.

Rochonzon, which he knew was the demon.

So, Heath wasn't able to do much in the way of helping with that first part. Fortunately, Tony didn't seem to need any help with it. He never ever looked at Heath during the whole ... speech? Oration? Seminar?

Heath wasn't quite sure...

No. Conjuration. That was the word he was looking for. Odd that they called this conjuring, when to Heath, "conjure" was something very, very different.

And this conjuring, it didn't seem to work.

Tony finished all that Latin, and the triangle looked just as empty as it had when they'd all entered the ritual chamber.

Silence reigned for a moment, spoiled only by the rumbling complaint of Heath's belly, which had been too long empty.

But if Rochonzon's failure to appear had disturbed Tony, Heath could see no sign. Tony just started in again, a shorter speech this time, punctuated by repeating the demon's name three time.

Still nothing.

That got a grimace out of Tony. He then hefted that rowan wand and pointed it at the triangle.

More Latin. Sounded vaguely threatening.

Finally, a response.

First thing Heath noticed was a little chill work its way through the room. Just enough at the back of his neck to send a shiver down his spine. Heath might have thought it was just him, but a moment later, DeAndre's shoulders moved in the same kind of shiver.

Of course, when a guy as big as DeAndre shivered, it looked like more of a production than it did on Heath.

Tony, though, didn't seem to notice. Except that his nostrils flared.

A moment later, Heath figured out why that reaction. He could smell it now too. Just a hint of sulfur in the air, under the smell of frankincense. Like someone on the other side of the door had a handful of rotten eggs.

Only then did Heath spot a change in the slight haze to the air. Little bits of frankincense smoke from around the room began to coalesce, coming together in the triangle.

At first, it seemed like a solid cloud of smoke. Not touchably solid, but solid in the sense that it was constrained to a sphere maybe a foot across.

Then the sphere shifted into the shape of a lion with the head of a bald man with huge, moonlike eyes and a gaping mouth filled with shark teeth.

It spoke in a voice like a thousand bats screeching all at once.

"Who dares?"

"I," Tony said, switching to English now.

Well, if nothing else, at least Heath would be able to *understand* the rest of the interaction.

"I am Father Antonio, priest of the Holy Catholic Church and Shield of the Protective Order of Saint Benedict."

Shield? Heath would have to remember to ask about that later.

Tony continued.

"By God the Father I call and constrain you, Rochonzon. By God the Son I call and constrain you, Rochonzon. By God the Holy Spirit I call and constrain you, Rochonzon."

The smoke shifted, and Rochonzon took the shape of a horse

standing upright, huge penis erect, though the horse's forelegs were the clawed talons of an eagle and its head was that of an alligator.

"Ah," Rochonzon said, and this time its voice sounded like incoming fog, faint, but insistent. "I see DeAndre McDaniels is here. Tell me, priest, have your brought me here to pay his debt?"

"I have not. I have—"

"Ah," Rochonzon continued, louder. Voice more like a distant foghorn now. "I sense Heath Cyr as well. Samigina sends his regards. He wants you to know that Randall Jason Aldis has yet to appear on the rolls of those who died in a state of sin."

"Maybe he got right with God before he kicked it," Heath said, the words all but coming out on autopilot. Oh, they were his words all right, but Randall Jason Aldis was a client — if a jackass — and Heath had no intention of coughing the boy up when Heath had gone to so much trouble to protect him in the first place.

"Do not speak to these others," Tony said, shooting Heath a warning glare. "Such as you have no right to address the sons of Adam. You may address me only because I have called you here."

"I may address DeAndre all I like," Rochonzon said. "You cannot stop that, priest. He and I are bound by a contract."

A long, snake-like tongue flicked out over the demon's alligator teeth. The fiend had managed to become more solid, and Heath had missed that. Not a good sign.

"In fact," Rochonzon turned to DeAndre. "Do you remember the exact terms of our arrangement, DeAndre?"

DeAndre did an admirable job of not looking. Though he had to hunch his shoulders a bit.

"You will confine your remarks to me, demon," Tony said, but Rochonzon pushed on before Tony could force the issue.

"You promised me lives, DeAndre. That guard was only the beginning. You promised me one human life every seven years, or I have the right to claim your life *and* your soul. Remember that, DeAndre?"

"The terms of your agreement are moot," Tony said, hefting the rowan wand. "I declare that deal null and void. *Deleantur ab initio.*"

"Ah, but that agreement is very much in effect, and DeAndre

here's next payment is late," Rochonzon said, and now its voice seemed to slither through the room as it shifted shapes again, now taking a serpentine body so long it pressed against every side of the triangle. Its head looked like something out of *Jurassic Park*, with a crest that flared to life when it continued speaking.

Also, Heath noted to his dismay that the demon had color now. Emerald green for its body and head, and bright orange for its crest.

"If you don't fulfill the terms, DeAndre. After I take your life and your soul. Do you remember what happens then?"

DeAndre's back stiffened. His hands clenched into fists.

"Your first born child, DeAndre. Remember that little clause? Didn't have one at the time, did you? Never thought you would. *But you do now.*"

And Heath got that sinking feeling in his gut that said this was all about to go horribly wrong.

———

"No!" DeAndre cried, whirling back around. His clenched hands came up as though he intended to fight the demon with his fists alone, if need be.

"*DeAndre Alan McDaniels*," Tony bellowed out, and in one of those oddly distant moments, Heath wondered when Tony had learned DeAndre's middle name.

Tony, however, kept talking.

"You will turn away from the demon *right now!*"

"Face me, DeAndre," Rochonzon taunted, and somehow the demon made those words sound like hissing. "Take me. Challenge me. Kill me if you can."

DeAndre took a step forward, murder in his eyes. He looked for all the world as though he intended to do just what the demon said.

"Deal with the demon," Heath said to Tony. "Leave DeAndre to me."

To Tony's credit, he didn't hesitate.

Tony started spouting Latin again, but Heath's focus was entirely on DeAndre. And Heath never hesitated to turn new knowledge to application.

"DeAndre Alan McDaniels," Heath said in *listen-to-me* tones. Not a true compulsion like the *compelling gaze*, but those tones had a way of cutting right through all the garbage and internal monolog going on in a person's head. Make sure they heard what Heath was saying and gave it proper attention.

Heath could only hope that tone would cut through the influence of the demon. He'd never used it this way.

But this was the best Heath could do right now. He needed eye contact for the *compelling gaze*, and he certainly couldn't risk stepping out of the circle to apply any compulsion oils to DeAndre.

Tony had never specifically told Heath not to step out of the circle, but he was still pretty sure it was a bad idea. And though Heath could have soaked a packet with compulsion oil — even *bend over* oil, which was the strongest of its kind — and thrown it hard enough to nail DeAndre in the face, he figured that might count as breaking the circle. Or both circles. Either way, a really bad idea.

Heath didn't know the rules of this kind of ceremonial crap, but it all seemed to be stuff written by the kind of people who dedicated themselves to the letter of the law, not the spirit.

Those were probably bid ideas anyway. DeAndre needed to turn away from the demon of his own free will, or there might be consequences.

So all Heath could do was keep talking in *listen-to-me* tones and hope that he got through to DeAndre.

"You look at me right now," Heath said. "You turn your focus right over here to me. 'Cause I've got something to tell you, conjure man to conjure man, and if you can't look at me right now, then you aren't conjure man enough to hear it. You hear what I'm telling you, DeAndre? I'm not sure you're a good enough root worker to grab hold of your focus and turn it wherever you want it. Is that right? Is what I see here all you are? Are you just another client? Just another kid off the street with no will of his own? Just a sucker for any little ghostie with enough juice to make a bunch of incense smoke look like a snake?"

Heath held up his hands in a shrug, and flattened his lips, but he held tight to that *listen-to-me* tone.

"Well, DeAndre? You conjure man enough to look at me right now?"

DeAndre's raised fists started to shake. His whole bald head glistened with sweat.

Took a major feat of willpower, but DeAndre turned to look at Heath. And when he did, DeAndre lowered his fists.

That was all Heath needed. The moment Heath caught his eyes, Heath focused down into the *compelling gaze*.

He could feel the turmoil in DeAndre's head. Practically see the backdoor that this demon had built for itself. Easy, instant access.

But Heath hadn't snuck into DeAndre's mind by any backdoor or window. He'd barged right in through the front door and gotten into the host's face.

Heath poured pure willpower into his words now.

"Ain't nobody else here but me, DeAndre. You got that? You and me, we're the only people down here in this big stone chamber. Oh, I've got Tony on speaker phone, so you might hear his voice, and you can answer him if he asks you a question. But only if he asks you a question. You understand me?"

Now, under normal circumstances, DeAndre — as a conjure man in his own right — might have been difficult to trap in the *compelling gaze*. But right then, Heath had already been warming him up with *listen-to-me* tones. Plus, poor DeAndre had just had his mind abused by a demon and hadn't had a chance to recover.

What was more, if Heath was honest with himself, it probably helped that Heath had only good intentions right then. The *compelling gaze* could be a powerful thing, but it seemed a mind always seemed to know if Heath was intending to use it in way that could hurt the target.

Not that Heath used the *compelling gaze* that way. Or all that much at all, really. But he'd noticed that if he used it to help someone, it always seemed to be easier.

So DeAndre, he looked on Heath with the kind of steadfast focus usually only seen on a stage during some kind of comedy hypnosis act.

DeAndre's deep voice sounded slightly hollow when he said, "I understand, Heath."

"Keep your eyes on me now," Heath said, "don't you worry about what I'm looking at."

"All right."

And Heath turned to see how things were going.

Tony was glowing.

Literally.

The monk stood tall and strong, and a faint white glow seemed to emanate from his skin and clothes.

Now, Heath was used to seeing his share of supernatural phenomena. Yes, most of the time it meant he had his spirit eyes open and was seeing things of a more subtle, ephemeral nature. But Heath kept himself in the kind of synchronicity with the ebbs and flows of the universe that he could see plenty these days, even without opening his spirit eyes.

More than he wanted to see, most of the time. But then, the conjure path was like that. For every one thing of beauty, there were probably a dozen horrors waiting. After all, the world was a dangerous place.

But the sight of Tony glowing like some saint out of the Bible, that was one of those rarer beautiful sights.

He'd dropped his rowan wand in there somewhere. And instead he had his arms stretched out to the sides, as though he were a living representation of Christ crucified.

Tony was still spouting the Latin nonstop, but now it sounded like one of the prayers Heath had heard in the church his family went to back in New York. One of those churches that considered some of the decisions made at Vatican II ... optional. Still did the mass in Latin, for example.

And Rochonzon, that old demon didn't look quite so scary now. Rochonzon had lost its color, and most of its coherence. It was in the form of a giant spider now, with a scorpion's tail, but two of its legs were broken, as was one of its pincers.

Even better, it was a spider made of gray smoke, and that broken pincer was leaking smoke at an impressive rate.

While Heath was watching, two more legs snapped.

"Yield!" the demon yelled at last, its voice sounding almost like a panicky teenage human. "I yield."

It shifted again, into the form of a dog with the head of a gibbon, and abased itself. "I yield to you, mighty conjurer."

"No," Tony said, and his voice seemed to echo in the small chamber. "It is not to me you yield, demon, but to your Creator. I am no conjurer here, but His servant, defending His children."

"Yes," Rochonzon whined. "What must I do to earn release from this torment?"

Torment? Just what had Tony been doing?

"You overreached yourself, demon. You demanded that which no mortal man can promise — the soul of another. Not even their own offspring. You have no claim on the child of DeAndre Alan McDaniels, and never did. Further, you have lost all claim to DeAndre Alan McDaniels. He has regretted his rash decision and returned to the fold. He is once more under the protection of the shepherds. By all rights, I could release this man from his debts to you, and still require you to fulfill your end of that ill-fated bargain."

"But—" the demon began, but Tony interrupted.

"But I will not. What I do instead is dissolve this bargain from its inception. By the authority vested in me by my Order, by the Church, and by our most merciful God above, I declare your bargain with DeAndre Alan McDaniels — including the man known to me as Papa Dusk — annulled. Not merely broken, but dissolved from its beginning. As of now, this bargain never existed."

"Agreed," Rochonzon said.

Heath couldn't help but wonder what would have happened if

Rochonzon had disagreed here. Was there an appellate court for the resolution of demon contracts?

"Then your purpose here is fulfilled. And for overreaching yourself, I confine you to Hell for a duration of no less than seven years and seven days. I do this in the name of the Father," — Tony sprinkled holy water that Heath hadn't realized he was holding — "in the name of the Son" — more holy water — "and in the name of the Holy Spirit." — more holy water — "*Get. Thee. Hence.*"

GONE. THE DEMON WAS GONE, AND NOW THAT RITUAL CHAMBER FELT larger.

Heath hadn't realized it, but the presence of Rochonzon had begun to make that huge stone chamber feel small. And now that it was gone — and Heath had no doubts that it was gone — that chamber felt almost as big as a football field.

It smelled better too. Heath hadn't realized how the sulfurous smell of the demon had grown stronger while it was here, but all of a sudden the sweet scent of frankincense was dominant again.

The air even felt cooler.

Tony wasn't glowing anymore. And the poor guy looked exhausted. Pale, and a little drawn.

"Hey," Heath said, stepped forward and putting a hand on his shoulder. "You all right?"

"I am," Tony said, nodding with a weak smile. "That ... takes a lot out of me though."

"Really?" Heath asked, more than a little surprised. "I figured that wasn't so much you as a higher power *through* you."

"Yes," Tony said, smiling wider, and that smile filled his eyes now too. "And if you think that's easy on a body, you've never had it happen."

"No, thank you," Heath said quickly. "So far I have managed to live my life as the only occupant of my skin, and I'd like very much to keep it that way."

"Heath," DeAndre said. "Heath. I don't... I..."

Heath glanced over and saw the big man frowning with his whole face. He was shaking his head a little too.

Oh. Right.

Heath snapped his fingers and released DeAndre from the *compelling gaze*. The big man's eyes rounded wide, as suddenly he could see Tony again, standing right where he'd been unable to see him a moment ago.

Unfortunate, that. Heath had told DeAndre to keep his eyes on Heath, but also that Heath and DeAndre were alone. That Tony was only present on the speakerphone. So DeAndre's mind tried to not see Tony while watching Heath. Which was fine, the ability of a mind to focus and edit what it sees can be quite impressive.

At least, everything was fine right up until Heath touched Tony.

There's only so much one should ask of the human mind.

DeAndre continued shaking his head. "Did you..."

DeAndre's fists came up, clenching and unclenching. "Did you use *compelling gaze* on me, motherfucker?"

"Yes, I did," Heath said, unrepentant. "And you should be damn glad you came to a conjure man strong enough to snatch your mind that way. Otherwise, you'd have stepped out of that circle and all Tony's effort would have been wasted."

DeAndre immediately looked chagrined. Hung his head and slumped his shoulders.

"Sorry about that," he said, and Heath was so shocked at the apology that he couldn't speak for a moment.

Tony was at no such loss.

"You have no reason to apologize. A demon had a direct line into your head. The circle and the blessings helped, but because you'd given that line of your own accord, our preparations could only do so much."

"God," DeAndre said, then flinched as though he'd given offense. "Sorry. It's just... My little girl. I never even thought. I'd forgotten all about..."

"Doesn't matter now," Tony said in a soothing tone. He stepped out of the circle and right up to DeAndre. He said some things then in a low voice that Heath couldn't hear.

But honestly, Heath didn't try. It just seemed too private.

"So," Heath said when the monk seemed to be finished. "I take it this part is done?"

"Absolutely," Tony said, smiling again. "DeAndre, that deal is as though it never happened." Tony shook his head then. "Well, almost. Time has not been undone, and so you are here with us, and not back in prison. But don't be surprised if some police detective catches a break on the cold case of the murder of that guard."

"I know," DeAndre said with a nod. "Worth it. I mean it."

"We're not done yet," Heath said, over the rumble of his empty stomach. "Papa Dusk, wherever he is, is going to figure out pretty quick that he's stopped getting his bennies from that bargain. And he's going to come looking for you."

Heath smiled. "That's where my part comes in."

"Think you'll need any help?" Tony asked, wavering just a little on his feet, but a determined look in his eye.

"Tony," Heath said with a laugh. "You look like you need a week's worth of sleep and about two pounds of prime rib before you're up to anything else."

"No doubt," DeAndre said, then grabbed Tony's hand and started pumping it. "And I want to buy that prime rib, when you're ready to eat it. Plus make a donation to your order. If you don't mind, that is."

"Both sound fine with me," Tony said, but DeAndre wasn't done. He was shaking his head with wonder as he continued shaking Tony's hand.

"I still can't believe it. A demon that badass and you just stomped him down. I couldn't have done that. Not even at my best. And I'm betting Heath couldn't have done it either. No offense."

"None taken," Heath said with a smile. "That's why I brought you to the experts in this field. I know where my limits are."

"Before you go thinking this was easy," Tony said, finally getting his hand back, "remember the situation. You came *here*, to the holiest site I could offer within two days' drive. You came downstairs into a ritual chamber that has seen more blessings than many churches. You came of your own volition, you brought your own regret for the sacrifice to the demon, and more importantly your willingness to repent that sin."

Tony drew a deep breath and let it out. "You stacked the deck in my favor. At least as much as you could. And *still*, I might have failed if Heath hadn't been able to keep you in that circle."

DeAndre blinked. "Heath, I..."

"Part of the service," Heath said, waving off whatever DeAndre was going to say. "Now, we should see about getting ready to deal with Papa Dusk."

Heath's stomach rumbled again.

"I'd say you need to see to lunch first," Tony said.

"No reason we can't do both," Heath said. "Besides, Colin ought to be done with his rant by now."

4

TONY MIGHT HAVE BEEN WILLING TO GO STRAIGHT OUT FOR A LATE lunch, but neither Heath nor DeAndre would hear of it. Both insisted on helping clean up the ritual chamber before leaving it.

That made Heath chuckle as they went about the task. Just another reason not to have a ritual chamber. If Heath did some root-work in his kitchen, all the had to do to clean up was the same kind of thing he'd've done to prepare the kitchen for lunch anyway.

Also, cleaning up gave Heath a chance to ask a question that had been bothering him.

"Tony, what did—"

"Don't name the demon," Tony said in a warning tone, as he re-locked that chest and slid it back under the altar.

Heath was now curious how Tony knew that he was about to use the demon's name, but that was secondary to the more important question.

"Well, the demon then," Heath said. "It said you were torturing it?"

"Of course," Tony said as he stood and gave the chamber a quick look-over to make sure they hadn't missed anything. They hadn't.

Even the smell of frankincense was fading to more of a background scent, overlaying the dry stone smell.

"I forced the demon to face the light of God," Tony said. "You must remember that this was not a fallen angel, but a demon unto itself. The fallen, faced with the light of God, might repent their ways and be forgiven. Demons don't have that option, as such — it's complicated — but they cannot stand in the light of God. It's too much for them."

"Can't take the righteous heat." DeAndre said with a smile.

"Exactly," Tony said, then frowned in thought. "DeAndre, when you said you would want to oppose demons—"

"Later for that conversation," Heath said quickly. "Right now we've got Papa Dusk to deal with. No splitting focus."

"Fair enough," Tony said.

And then they were done at last, and Tony led them back up out of that sub-sub-basement. Holy site full of blessings or not, Heath was more than happy to have less and less rock and earth over his head as he ascended the stairs behind Tony and DeAndre.

Though, admittedly, Heath wouldn't have minded preceding DeAndre. The big man had been sweating profusely in his expensive suit, and the odor was one Heath could have done without.

But then, Heath and Tony would probably have benefited from showers as well.

All of which just made the fresh air out behind the monastery that much sweeter when Tony led them outside again.

The sweet scent of Douglas firs, and the clean aromas of fresh earth and recently cut grass.

Here behind the monastery, the birds sang at least three different songs. Heath picked out meadowlarks, stellar jays and crows pretty quickly, but he thought there was a fourth bird song he wasn't quite catching.

All of these birds were happily singing in the canopy formed by the Douglas firs. Those trees grew tighter and thicker here than Heath was used to seeing them. And they formed a ring, in the center of which was an intricately carved white stone table, complete with benches.

Colin was already sitting at the table. And he looked as though he'd gotten that rant out of his system. He was smiling again, looking like the skinny white stoner he wasn't quite. Oh, he was skinny and white enough, but he never did touch drugs.

And yet, Heath still thought of Colin's look as stoner chic. Some habits of thought were a little too ingrained, it seemed.

"So," Colin said with a smile. "Got the demon on the run? Get thee behind me, Satan, and all that?"

"Every bit of it," Tony said, laughing now. He took the seat next to Colin, leaving the other side for DeAndre and Heath.

"Sorry about the rant," Colin said, his smile dipping. "Chaos magicians just piss me off."

"Figured that," DeAndre said, hands coming up. "Don't worry. I'll never accuse you of being one of them."

Colin snickered.

"Mind you," DeAndre continued, "I don't understand just what the hell you *do* do, or how you make it work."

"Goes both ways," Colin said, smirking at his double-entendre as he always did when he found an excuse to use those words. "I don't get how you and Heath do your thing."

"Could teach you," DeAndre said, making Heath sit a little straighter in surprise.

"Forget it," Colin said, shaking his head. "Might make me as grumpy and hostile as you two get."

Heath opened his mouth to make a remark about chaos magicians, but Tony raised an eyebrow at Heath, and instead Heath said, "I believe lunch was mentioned?"

"It should be along in a moment," Tony said.

And sure enough, a moment later two young monks in brown robes, with lengths of soft-looking brown cord as belts, came out carrying picnic baskets.

Neither monk looked old enough to shave, and apparently that included their heads, because they both had full heads of short, black hair. No tonsure for these two. At least, not yet. One of the monks had the same kind of olive skin tone that Tony did, but the other had more of a Latin American look to him.

"More novices?" Heath said, surprised, once the two young monks had set down the baskets and retreated. "Just how well is your order doing?"

"It's true," Tony said, "that many orders are drawing fewer and fewer new recruits. But, sadly, those who face problems of a supernatural nature seem to see their ranks swell daily."

"If you don't mind," DeAndre said, his deep voice gentle, "some day I'd love to hear the story of the event that brought you to the order, Brother Tony."

"And some day you might," Tony said with a smile. "But for right now, we have food to eat, and plans to make."

And with that, they broke out the food.

It was late afternoon by the time that "lunch" was finished.

The sun wasn't quite setting, but the sky to the west was starting to turn orange, and off to the east the first hints of oncoming night could just be made out past the canopy of Douglas firs. The air had picked up a little chill, but not enough to matter. Probably helped that the stone bench table had picked up some of the warmth from the diners, and was giving it back to them.

Most important, Heath was glad to say there'd been enough food. Colin alone seemed to have hollow places to store food secreted throughout his skinny body. The boy ate one whole fried chicken and loaf of bread all on his own.

Of course, in his defense, it was magnificent rye bread, and the monks seemed to have a good trick with the way they fried their chicken. Garlic and rosemary, and breading that got just the right amount of crispness to it, without being too thick.

Heath, of course, gave a good accounting for his own appetite, and DeAndre was a big man for a reason. Perhaps most surprising was the way that Tony had gone after his food as well.

But then, he'd been clear that his work down in that ritual chamber had taken more than a little bit out of him.

Fortunately, the monks of the Protective Order of Saint Benedict seemed to have an excellent sense of exactly how much they'd need. How much chicken, how much rye bread, how much salad, and how many brownies.

The brownies were the best part. If it weren't for the fact that Heath knew he was sitting on holy ground, he would have called them sinfully good.

Right then, though, it just wasn't a joke he was up to making.

Colin, of course, made the joke.

So, by the time they were ready to leave, Heath, DeAndre and Colin had eaten their fill, and drunk their fill of a fine, clear IPA that the monks brewed themselves.

What they had not done, alas, was hold anything like a useful war council.

The problem was simple. DeAndre had known nothing of conjure and rootwork until he started studying with Papa Dusk. And Papa Dusk played up the "man of mystery" angle, so that he might have been a charlatan, only barely keeping ahead of his student DeAndre. Or he might have been the biggest, nastiest conjure man this side of Heath's uncle.

They simply had no way to tell for certain.

Which made planning all the harder.

Also, making planning difficult, DeAndre kept coming back to questions about the Protective Order of Saint Benedict. Heath was starting to think that the big man was thinking seriously of committing himself to the Order.

Colin seemed to be thinking it too, to judge from the looks he kept shooting Heath.

Heath did step away from the lunch table long enough — and far enough — to be able to give Nariko a call. He only got her voice mail, but he made sure to tell her about the call he'd gotten from Mrs.

Tachibana, and everything he could think of about that call that might be important. Including what time the call came in, and how long it lasted before he hung up on her.

The timing details probably wouldn't have mattered to Heath, but they might to Nariko.

Finally, though, the late lunch was finished, and it was time to leave the monastery.

"All right," Heath said, coming to his feet. He rubbed his hands together. "Now, I think we're all agreed that Papa Dusk must know by now that his deal's been nixed, right?"

Three faces, nodding agreement, but curious about where he was going with this.

"Any way he'd be able to tell that it was nixed from the outset?" Heath looked at Tony. "What did you say? Destroyed *ab initio*?"

"Yes," Tony said, "But I don't know if that will be clear to Papa Dusk. Depends on what he was getting out of it."

"You're sure you don't know that?" Heath asked DeAndre.

DeAndre shook his head. "I've been wracking my brains, but apart from getting out and getting some money, I don't remember."

"Getting some money?" Heath's tone was sharp, because that information was new. "You didn't mention that before."

"I didn't?" DeAndre shook his head. "Sorry. Hard to focus on that memory. Probably a side effect of, well, that demon messing with my head."

"Partially," Tony said, "but also because the deal was dissolved the way it was. If the deal never existed, you'll have trouble recalling the details."

"Will Papa Dusk?" Heath asked.

"Probably," Tony said, but he was moving his head back and forth as though he wasn't sure of that himself. "Tough to say. DeAndre was here when the change was made, and his connection was severed immediately. In Papa Dusk's case, it's more likely to fade slowly. Unless he's a sufficiently savvy practitioner to notice a small, growing change immediately."

"Assume he is," Colin said. "That's the safer path."

"True," Heath said. "So. If it were me, and I knew that deal got undone, first thing I'd do is send a helper to come check on you, DeAndre. Figure out where you were and what you were up to."

"Agreed," DeAndre said, coming to his feet. "I may try to eat the little jab myself."

"What did you call it?" Heath said quickly.

"Jab," DeAndre said. "You know, like a quick punch? That's what Papa Dusk always called little spirit helpers. I know you like that 'little ghostie' thing, but ... what?"

DeAndre must have seen the careful look on Heath's face. Certainly Colin had figured it out by now, and maybe Tony, but DeAndre, he didn't have the right background, and he hadn't exactly been hanging out with Heath lately.

"The word," Heath said, "is *djab*. And it's a Vodou term." Heath started tapping his chin, trying to think of another term to check on. Shook his head. "Think, DeAndre. Did Papa Dusk ever use any other expressions you never really hear in conjure work?"

DeAndre had to think about that one, and it looked like work. Heath almost wanted to let him off the hook. The poor guy had been through a lot lately. Still, this was important information.

And besides, Heath wasn't *quite* willing to look past their history together.

"Only one I can think of," DeAndre said, frowning and shaking his head. "He used to say 'pen' sometimes when talking about magic. But I just thought that was because we were in the pen. You know?"

"Pen?" Heath said, watching his pronunciation carefully. "Or *pwen*?"

DeAndre blinked in surprise. "Yeah. Yeah, that second thing. How did you say it?"

"*Pwen*," Heath said again, a slight sinking feeling in his stomach.

"*Pwen*," DeAndre repeated. "Yeah, that was it. How did you know?"

"Another term from Vodou." Heath shook his head. "All right. Well. If he was calling up a demon instead of working with the Lwa, then he's no *houngan*. Probably not even a *bokor*."

"Which means..." DeAndre said.

"Not a Vodou priest, or a ... Vodou sorcerer. More or less." Heath shook his head. This was no time for long explanations. "That's good, far as it goes, but I'm not sure what it means yet. Could just be that he picked up the terms locally where he learned what he knew."

Heath frowned, surprised he hadn't ask this question before. "Where did you do time together?"

"Joliet," DeAndre said. "In Illinois."

"What does that tell you, Heath?" Colin asked.

"Nothing, unfortunately," Heath admitted. "I was hoping it was someplace steeped enough in Vodou that he might have picked up the terms casually. But Illinois? Chicago might have enough ... practitioners" — no point in saying *serviteurs*, they wouldn't know what it meant — "for that to happen, in the right neighborhoods, but most of the state wouldn't."

"Still," Colin said. "Snagging whatever he sends for us. That'll help us figure it out, right?"

"That's the plan," Heath said, noting that Colin had said "sends for us" and not "sends for DeAndre."

"Won't reach him here," Tony said, confidence in his voice. "The grounds of his monastery provide sanctuary in many forms. One of the most important is that we ward strongly against detection."

"Nice," DeAndre said.

"The monastery," Heath said, "but not the whole cemetery, is that right?"

"Of course," Tony said. "A ward that big, over a place accessible to the public, would draw attention, which would defeat the purpose."

"Your Lexus," Heath said to DeAndre. "Papa Dusk's little ghostie will track you as far as that, and be waiting for you there."

"You have a plan, don't you?" Colin said, then turned to DeAndre and added. "You can always tell by that little sparkle in his eye."

Heath chuckled. No point in denying it.

HEATH LEFT TONY, DEANDRE AND COLIN ALL WAITING BACK BY THE stone picnic bench. Each wanted to come along, and Heath refused each for different reasons.

DeAndre, of course, couldn't come along, or it would ruin Heath's good work. The little ghostie — or whatever exactly it was that Papa Dusk had sent — would bypass Heath's little distraction and shoot straight for the real thing.

Tony, Heath refused, for a couple of reasons. One, despite the fortification of a good, if late, lunch, Tony still looked too much like a dead man walking for Heath's taste. Heath wanted that monk to get more rest before throwing himself back into the line of fire.

Admittedly, Heath couldn't stop Tony, if his heart was set on coming along, but Heath didn't want to encourage him either.

Colin, well, by all rights, Colin could have come along if he really wanted to. Colin had his own protections, and was practitioner enough to hold his own if anything about Heath's plan blew up.

Still, Heath was the one getting paid to take this risk. Colin was only along to be sociable. Well, and out of his seemingly limitless curiosity. That boy would risk his life and his soul to see something new.

And Heath and DeAndre getting along sure counted as something new. To say nothing of Colin's strange fascination with watching Heath work.

Of course, Colin probably wouldn't have admitted it, but he was likely also along out of concern for Heath. Heath had, on occasion, been known to find himself in deeper trouble than he could get himself out of. And with Nariko out of town, Colin might have been watching over Heath on her behalf.

Heath might have bitched about that, but the way the last couple of months had gone, he couldn't deny that having ready help available was proving to be a good thing, more and more.

Still, none of those were good enough reasons right then for Heath to let Colin come along. Whatever *djab* Papa Dusk had called up to find DeAndre might also have been sent to teach the big man a lesson.

Yes, Heath knew a thing or two about dealing with wild spirits, and aggressive spirits, but still. Plan or no plan, Heath couldn't be entirely sure how much trouble he was walking into. And he wasn't about to let Colin face that trouble over nothing more than curiosity and friendship.

So Heath was on his own as he made his slow, casual way back across the cemetery from the monastery. It was a pretty good walk, and empty enough that the late afternoon air was downright peaceful.

Cemeteries could be like that for Heath. Sometimes they felt peaceful. Calm. Like they were welcoming places. Other times they could be as raucous as a nightclub with a happening DJ.

All depended on a number of factors.

But right then, the late afternoon air was cool. The sky was a darkening blue, still turning a lovely orange out west where it was starting to set. The grass was mown close, but not recently enough to have much impact on the scent Heath was still getting from the Douglas firs behind him.

This particular cemetery, here in Lake Oswego, was little more than a series of hills. Pretty good workout, if Heath were to take it quickly enough. Or smooth, if he went over to the gravel-edges asphalt of the driving path that cut through the cemetery in loops.

One thing the cemetery lacked though. Mausoleums. Heath had loved the mausoleums of New Orleans cemeteries when he was a kid. Back before he even noticed very many of the restless spirits that tended to roam around New Orleans cemeteries.

He missed those. He'd have to start checking around the local cemeteries for the ones with good mausoleums. Might even be a good place for a conversation with Ghede Brav, about returning that flask.

Heath was approaching the parking lot when he pulled his thought back to the present. Only about three cars left in that lot. Two Subarus with Oregon plates, and DeAndre's Lexus LX 450, parked off by itself in a corner.

Heath stopped and opened up his spirit eyes just before his feet touched asphalt. Connections and associations were tricky things.

Depending on what was waiting, it might be able to sense every inch of the parking lot at the same time, but not be able to stretch its sense five inches into the grass.

The grass, after all, was not the parking lot.

Spirits could be funny like that.

Heath, however, had no such restrictions. He opened up his spirit eyes and took a good look around.

Dead boy floating over near one of the Subarus. Next to a green Outback. Dead boy looked to have been about twenty-one when he died. Had some kind of uniform on, but from here Heath couldn't tell what.

Didn't matter. Someone was here to visit the dead boy, and he was trying to visit them right back.

Heath watched as the Outback fired up and pulled out. The dead boy followed the car as far as the edge of the parking lot, but got stuck there as the car left.

Borders. That was how they worked sometimes.

Heath took a moment to utter a prayer of blessing for the dead, his own effort to do some good for the poor stuck dead boy. And Heath made a mental note to tell Tony about the dead boy. No doubt one of the priests would want to come lay him to rest. And better that this be done soon, before some ... less scrupulous practitioner came along and bound that spirit to a bottle or something.

Heath had just such a bottle in his left hand. Little thing. Couldn't hold more than maybe four ounces of liquid. And it was a dark blue glass, decorated with just the right kind of symbols on the outside. Written in black Sharpie.

Of course, this bottle didn't have dirt from the dead boy's grave, or any of the three or four other elements necessary to snag the dead boy.

But then, that wasn't why Heath was here.

Heath's bottle had a few choice herbs in it, along with a couple of drops of special oils. And most important, several drops of DeAndre's sweat.

Oh, did DeAndre hesitate before handing that over. Made Heath grin just to think about it.

But DeAndre knew what Heath had in mind, so he couldn't really object. Not unless he wanted to do without Heath's help.

Heath looked past the dead boy now, all the way down to DeAndre's Lexus.

Sure enough, there was a little ghostie floating around it right now. Not much form to it. Little more than a collection of eyes, ears, and noses.

At least, right now. Once it found what it was looking for, it might well shift into a combat shape. Assuming it had one.

In any event, this little ghostie wasn't any of DeAndre's. Or, if it were, it hadn't been there earlier. Heath didn't count it likely. DeAndre was smart enough to say something, if he'd been expecting one of his spirits to show up.

Wasn't one of Colin's either, for the same reason. And Tony, of course, didn't keep spirits this way.

So that pretty much meant it was one of Papa Dusk's, here to find DeAndre. Maybe to ask some questions. Maybe to exact a little payback.

Tough to tell from here.

Heath readied his spirit bottle and stepped onto the asphalt.

Bingo. That little ghostie's head came up as though it had just heard the dinner bell.

The ghostie shifted into a collection of claws and talons and came speeding straight at Heath.

Heath held the bottle in front of him.

The little ghostie came winging right into it, certain of finding its prey.

Heath popped the cork on the bottle. Smiled. Tossed the bottle into the air and caught it again.

"Easy peasy," he muttered.

Then he heard the applause.

5

HEATH STOOD BY HIMSELF JUST INSIDE THE EDGE OF THE PARKING LOT OF that cemetery in Lake Oswego. Backpack slung over his right shoulder. Newly capped spirit bottle in his hands.

The sun was only just really starting to set. The sodium lights above the parking lot hadn't lit up yet, and the afternoon had taken on that shadowless aspect that twilight got sometimes.

As though maybe everything was in just a hint of dim shadow, so none of the shadows stood out. Everything looked a little extra crisp. The few clouds rolling through the sky. The Douglas firs between the cemetery and the main road, all only just swaying in the cool, fir-scented September breeze.

Cars along the main road added a buzzing undercurrent to the sound of the breeze through the trees.

And overlaying that sound, the kind of slow, building clap of someone who was either very impressed, or very sarcastic. No way to tell from just the sound.

Heath looked around, and saw someone watching from over by the funeral home at the near end of the parking lot.

This was an old man. Somewhere between three and four times

Heath's age. His long, natty hair had long since gone gray, and his chocolate skin had deep wrinkles around the eyes, mouth and throat.

He was a skinny man, and short, but his shoulders were back and his back was straight. He wore baggy jeans that hung on him. Might have fallen if not for the wide leather belt he wore. Long sleeved shirt with a color. Hard to be sure of the color from where he stood, but Heath thought it was red. That might be important, depending on who exactly this man was.

And Heath had his suspicions.

The man stood not more than a few inches over five feet, and Heath doubted he weighed much more than a hundred pounds soaking wet.

But his hands looked rough and calloused. And not all the lines on his face were put there by nature. Looked as though he had a couple of small scars on his cheeks, and around his eyes.

The man stopped clapping.

"Nice job," he said. "Really. I must say. I mean, if it were me, and I was out here looking to put the grab on a *djab*, I would have gone for the dead boy down by the driveway. But seeing as how you must have had the right kind of bait to catch the one you caught there, I'm guessing you knew exactly what you were doing. Didn't you now?"

"Speaking of guessing," Heath said, cocking his head to one side. "I'm guessing you must be the man they call Papa Dusk."

"In the flesh," Papa Dusk said with a broad smile and a bow. When he came back up he added. "For a little while longer, anyway. And you, you *must* be this Heath Cyr I've been hearing so much about."

"Oh?" Heath said, trying to cover his actual surprise by faking surprise half-heartedly. "Been asking around about me?"

"Oh, I know a few people in this area. Pretty much any port you're going to find, you'll run across a few people who owe favors to Papa Dusk."

"Big claim," Heath said, "but I only just heard about you today."

"Some of us don't like the attention." Papa Dusk lit a cigar then, and started strolling closer. "Some of us, in fact, go well out of our way to avoid attention."

"Is that right?" Heath smiled. "Far enough to offer up a human life to a demon to help you hide? Is that it?"

All the humor melted out of Papa Dusk's voice, and what was left was pure anger.

"Where is he? Where is that cheating bastard?"

"Well, if you're referring to a certain demon, I think you'll find he's not available to answer your calls. For a few years, anyway."

The made Papa Dusk narrow his eyes at Heath through a long, slow puff on his cigar.

"Man," Heath said through a lopsided grin, "if that cigar and nickname are supposed to impress me, they don't. I've spoken in person to Ghede Brav and Baron Samedi. Not to mention Papa Legba. You may call yourself Papa and you might throw around words like *djab*, but I'm betting you know less about real Vodou than William Seabrook."

Bit of a test, that statement. Most people these days didn't know who William Seabrook was. Or rather, had been, since the man had been dead for decades.

Unfortunately, he was also responsible for the book best known for bringing zombies to Hollywood. Some called his view of Vodou generous for its time, but Heath still considered it paternalistic and slanted.

Papa Dusk recognized the reference. Snorted.

"Maybe I'll talk to Kalfou about you," Papa Dusk said. "Maybe I'll go back to my *houmfo* and set something after you. What do you say to that?"

As though this man had a temple in the area.

"I say there are three active *humfos* in the greater Portland area, and you aren't attached to any of them. What's more, I don't believe for a moment that you're a *bokor*, much less a *houngan*." Heath shook his head. "I think you're a conjure man trying to play up the mystery angle by throwing in Vodou references you don't really understand."

"Well, that sounds to me like you're challenging me, boy."

"Maybe I am, maybe I'm not," Heath said with a shrug. "Depends on you. See, far as I'm concerned, you and me can let bygones be bygones. It's no skin off my nose if you play at Vodou. I'll let the real *serviteurs* deal with you. They will sooner or later."

Papa Dusk snorted, but Heath wasn't finished.

"The only thing keeping us from going our separate ways is your little trouble with DeAndre McDaniels."

"So you *do* know where that bastard is."

"Maybe," Heath said with a smile. "But why do you care?"

"I taught that punk bitch everything he knows. And we had a deal. I don't know how he broke it, but he did. Everything's going wrong. Everything's—"

"Hey," Heath said, hands coming up, one showing the bottle as a reminder that Heath had already overcome one thing Papa Dusk did today. "You tricked him, and we both know it. You made him pay the full freight for not only whatever *he* got out of that deal, but whatever *you* got out of that deal too."

"It was fair," Papa Dusk insisted. "I was the only one who could get him what he wanted. Only right that I get paid for my efforts. You work for free, conjure man?"

"I do not," Heath said. "But I work for a fair price. And I don't constrain my clients the way you constrained DeAndre. Honestly. You had him working the root, but he couldn't affect any legal matters without your aid? Subtle, but only because he was ignorant enough not to know that at least a fifth of all the conjure work done in this world is done to affect court cases, lawsuits and all that crap."

Heath shook his head. "You needed DeAndre to pay the price you didn't want to pay. You set that poor bastard up to keep murdering people, all so you could ... what exactly did you get out of this, anyway? Aside from hiding from the law and any other enemies you had. Money? Girls? Money *and* girls? Or do you actually have more intricate needs than the basics? Things you weren't conjure man enough to get on your own?"

"None of your goddamn business."

"Fine," Heath said with a shrug. "Truth is, I don't care. You tricked DeAndre into doing something he didn't really understand. I got him out of that trick. That's all that we have here. Far as I'm concerned, you two are even now and you should go your separate ways."

Heath ratcheted up his smile a notch. "Now, doesn't that sound like a better option than fighting me here in a cemetery parking lot?"

"That's the way it has to be, huh?" Papa Dusk said with a slow shake of his head. "The only way I'm going to find DeAndre is through you, is it? You better think that over, boy. I've been working the root for decades longer than you've been alive."

"Yeah, yeah," Heath said, dropping his backpack down to the asphalt. "You've had more years on the planet, I don't doubt that. But years alone do not a conjure man make. And if you were as badass as you try to come off, you'd've gone straight to DeAndre, even if he were hiding in the depths of hell."

"Fine," Papa Dusk said. Then spat off to one side. Then shrugged through a deep breath. "I got no beef with you. And maybe it's time I let DeAndre go his own way. I've figured out plenty since I got out of Joliet. Maybe I don't need a deal that evil to keep living the way I like."

He held out one hand. "Shake, and let's part on good terms."

Heath started laughing.

***

HEATH AND PAPA DUSK WERE THE ONLY ONES STANDING THERE IN THE parking lot of that Lake Oswego cemetery. So there was no one nearby to hear the ringing of Heath's loud, sincere laughter at the offer he'd just gotten from Papa Dusk.

Papa Dusk's frown came back, and it gained an order of magnitude in its severity.

"Oh," Papa Dusk said, and his voice trembled with anger. "So you're too good to shake hands with me? Is that it, boy?"

Heath kept laughing.

"Maybe I ought to—" Papa Dusk started, but Heath cut in over him.

"Stop," Heath said, slapping his knee with one hand. "Stop. I can't take it."

Papa Dusk frowned even deeper, and narrowed his eyes. He stabbed the air at Heath with his cigar. "Boy, I'm warning you—"

"Just how stupid do you think I am?" Heath said, now that he'd found enough breath. "Really? I'm supposed to believe you — *you* — are offering me a sincere handshake and a chance to part on good terms. For the sake of all that's holy, man, you *murdered a man to summon a demon*. And you made someone else pay the price. You and I both know you aren't going to walk away without either getting more than a pound of flesh out of DeAndre, or getting your ass kicked. Those are the only two options here."

Papa Dusk held out his hand once more to shake. "I'm offering you my hand, and you slap it away?"

"Yeah, yeah," Heath said, shaking his head, still chuckling. "Turn that hand toward the light, if you're ever so sincere."

Papa Dusk's brow wrinkled down further than nature had done to it already. "What are you trying to say?"

"I'm trying to say that you've probably laid tricks all around DeAndre's Lexus, not to mention on every one of the door handles, and the engine block, if you could get to it. Probably the tires too."

Heath smiled nice and wide. "And I have absolutely no doubt you've got a trick in your hand right now. A packet maybe, or a tiny pin coated with the right kind of oil to go with whatever you'd say if I was stupid enough to shake your hand."

Papa Dusk just gazed at Heath for a moment, while he smoked.

Heath let his smile melt away. Gave Papa Dusk a very serious look.

"Walk away," Heath said. "I don't want to fight you. There's no need for it. You played a trick. It got undone. Move the fuck on."

Papa Dusk started nodding. A slow, but steady gesture that continued through another long puff on his cigar.

Papa Dusk blew the smoke at Heath. Heath ducked under it and backed up a few steps, back onto the grass. He still picked up the scent of cheap tobacco, but he was confident that was all he picked up.

Nevertheless, Papa Dusk smiled.

"Yeah," Papa Dusk said. "You know not to shake my hand. Might just drag you down to hell with me."

Heath shook his head. "You're bastardizing what they say about the Baron. And I'm not afraid to shake your hand. I'm just not stupid enough to fall for an obvious trick."

"Maybe not," Papa Dusk said. "But are you sure you're up to a fair fight? You're not bad, boy. And you look as though you might have enough caution to live to a ripe old age, if you don't go around doing stupid things like challenging your betters."

"Leave DeAndre McDaniels in peace."

"Can't do it," Papa Dusk said. "I'm sure you know how much our reputations are worth, given what we do."

Heath smiled. "And here I thought you liked to stay hidden, Papa Dusk. Hidden men have no reputations to worry about."

"Yes," Papa Dusk said through a sigh that sounded sincerely sad, "they do. It's just that while you're name springs readily to the lips of certain types of people, mine is spoken of in whispers. Spoken in fear. People don't want to come to me for *baths* or *candles* or *spells*. People are afraid they'll meet me. They'll give me things to not hurt them."

Papa Dusk shook his head. "I like my privacy. But I like my fear too."

"Well," Heath said, "then I guess there's no other way."

"You're sure you won't just give me DeAndre? You like the guy that much?"

"He's a better man than I thought, but then that's not saying a lot." Heath shook his head. "But he's a client. So you can't have him."

"Piss poor conjure man he turned out to be," Papa Dusk said, "if he has to hire someone else to do his fighting for him."

"Well," Heath said, even though he knew that deep down, he half-agreed, "he didn't exactly know too much while he was studying with you. And since you put a lock on him to keep him from working any legal spells, it seems to me you might have left a backdoor connection open. Just in case you needed it."

"If I had that, why'd I have to come in person?"

"Wasn't sure you would," Heath said. "Figured you might have been able to rebuild it. That you're here tells me the backdoor connection was forged at the same time as you made your sacrifice to the demon. In fact, I'm willing to bet that it was part of the same ritual."

Heath smiled. "I'm betting that when that deal gone unmade, your direct connection went bye-bye. Didn't it?"

"Damn," Papa Dusk said with a slow shake of his head. "You do have potential, boy. Don't waste it. Don't make me kill you here and now."

"Forgive me if I don't just lay down and die," Heath said, "but I'm not giving you DeAndre either."

"All right then," Papa Dusk frowned and shook his head one more time. "Death it is."

And before Heath could throw the trick he'd snuck into his hand, or even make a witty comeback, he was under attack.

SOMETHING LEAPT RIGHT ONTO HEATH'S BACK. IT WAS A SPIRIT OF SOME kind. Must have approached from a blind angle. And it dug spirit claws right into him. Clamped its spirit jaws right down around his head.

Fortunately for Heath, the thing couldn't just bite right through him and kill him. Maybe it could have to most people. But though the baseline defenses Heath walked around with might not have been enough to stop this thing from attacking, they were at least enough to keep it from killing him outright.

Unfortunately for Heath, this attack still hurt like hell.

He dropped the trick in his one hand, and the spirit bottle in the other, letting out a cry of pain.

Those spirit claws raking his back felt like lava burning right down into his skin and settling in, burning deeper and deeper in a slow, relentless progression. And all the while, those claws kept raking more runnels in Heath's back.

And those jaws, they must have had row after row after row of long, sharp teeth, the way they felt like they were digging into Heath's skull and jaw. And they were burning every bit as hot as those claws were.

The world was a blinding swirl of pain. A cyclone of pain, and Heath wasn't quite in the eye. Oh, no. The eye might have been a moment of respite. Heath was trapped just at the outer edge, whirling and whirling through the pain just about as fast as pain could carry him.

And Heath was having a hell of a time trying to get any kind of grasp on much of anything. Any kind of anchor that might give him even a fraction of a moment's break from the pain. Just long enough for him to maybe get his bearings and do something about it.

His heart was pounding so fast it made his limbs shake. He couldn't stop himself from making this keening sound that drowned out whatever gloating thing Papa Dusk was saying.

That was when Heath heard a battle cry of some kind. Sounded like "Hoo-rah!" or something close to it. Hard to be sure. It wasn't a verbal sound anyway. It was more like a mental cry of some sort, intense enough to reach him through the pain.

Another spirit barreled hard into the side of that thing trying to take a big bite out of Heath's head. All of a sudden those jaws snapped away, and those claws missed.

Might have only been a moment, but it was enough for Heath.

He dove straight forward into Papa Dusk. Not with his arms wide for a tackle or anything. Heath was no football player. No, Heath dove forward and barreled his shoulder into the old man and sent him backwards onto the asphalt.

Heath twisted as he fell, determined not to come within reach of Papa Dusk and whatever trick he had lying ready in his hand.

Martial Arts was never Heath's thing. His attempt at a roll might have been awkward under the best of circumstances, and after dealing with seconds of blindingly intense pain, it wasn't even that good.

Still, Heath managed not to bang his head. And he may have given his poor body a few bumps and bruises, but under the echo of the pain he'd just been enduring, he couldn't even feel them yet.

Heath quickly pulled his back-up plan out of his shirt pocket and threw it down to break on the ground, scattering herbs and oils right there among the remnants of old gas and oil in the parking lot.

Heath hadn't been sure of what would be waiting out by the Lexus. And while he figured it *most likely* wasn't anything more dangerous than a simple watcher, he knew there was a strong possibility that Papa Dusk would have sent something big and bad. An assassin-type of spirit, as it were.

Say, like something with the kind of claws and jaws that could burn their way right into a man's soul.

And so Heath wanted to make sure he had a way to get such a spirit right where he wanted it.

And sure enough, the moment that bottle broke open, the spirit monster flew straight into it, away from whatever it had been fighting.

The monster wove around, up and down through the asphalt and into the air, but it couldn't get away. It was good and caught, as though it were a bear trap.

And now that Heath could see it, the spirit looked kind of like a bear. One of those great big grizzlies, if it had been horribly mutated by chemical runoff. Looked to Heath like a nature spirit of some sort, that Papa Dusk had bound to serve him.

Papa Dusk was swearing. He was on the ground and rubbing the back of his head, but his attention was all on the spirit Heath had trapped.

Now that Heath was looking for it, he could see the bonds. Just faintly around the throat and limbs of the bear spirit. They connected to Papa Dusk like a leash.

Heath fished a penknife out of the pockets of his cargo shorts, and a small vial of a special uncrossing and unbinding oil he made from his own recipe of lemon balm, hyssop, salt, five-finger grass, eucalyptus, and a couple of secret things he didn't talk about.

"What are you..." Papa Dusk started to ask, but stopped talking and hurried to his feet.

Heath oiled up the blade.

"No!" Papa Dusk cried.

But Papa Dusk wasn't fast enough.

Heath brought the blade down on those spirit bindings as he prayed aloud, "Whatever you loose on Earth shall be loosed in Heaven!"

And Heath cut the spirit bear free from Papa Dusk.

"No!" Papa Dusk cried out again, and started frantically digging for something in his pockets.

The spirit bear turned to look at Papa Dusk.

And it broke free of Heath's spirit trap.

The bear roared so loud it was almost painful in Heath's head, and it leapt onto Papa Dusk. Ripping into him with its claws. Worrying at his head with its jaws.

And Papa Dusk was not a young, vibrant man, like Heath.

"Sir," a voice said, and Heath turned to see the dead boy standing there. The uniform was plainly one of the United States Marines. He was also bleeding spirit stuff from several claw wounds. "Sir, should I save him too? I mean, he set that thing on you, but—"

"If it's what you really want to do, I won't stop you," Heath said. "But you should know he enslaved that spirit against its will, and he forced it to do things against its nature. Things it didn't want to do. That's why it looks so torn up the way it does. If you ask me, the spirit bear should have its chance for revenge. If Papa Dusk is as strong as he likes to say, he'll survive long enough to drive it off. Then I'll make sure he goes away and leaves us in peace."

"But..." the dead marine started, but then grimaced and shook his head.

Heath turned, to see the spirit bear running off on its own. And there on the parking lot asphalt, lay Papa Dusk. His eyes were open in shock, and he wasn't moving.

6

———

"HEATH!"

That was Colin's voice, yelling from back across the cemetery. Heath whirled. Focused. Colin, only just visible in the fading light of day, running flat out across the rolling hills, faster than a skinny boy like him should have been able to cover ground.

Tony loped behind Colin, nowhere near as fast.

DeAndre brought up the rear, and Heath almost lost a moment laughing at the sight of the big man in the expensive suit, running through a graveyard as though death itself were on his tail.

But Heath had something more important to do just then. So he waved to let them know he was all right, and they could slow to a walk.

Heath turned back to the dead marine, still bleeding spirit stuff from the dozens of cuts he'd gotten fighting the spirit bear. The sight made Heath's own wounds ache as though they'd carried through to his body, instead of stopping at a subtler form of his essence.

Heath dug into his backpack for the portable saucepan incense censer he called the bedpan. Its bed of salt had a coal all ready to go, and Heath lit it with a match, then poured a little blend of incense from a ready packet in his shirt pocket. The scent of allspice, cinnamon, and a couple of other herbs filled the chilling air.

Heath waved the censer under his own nose, then began brushing smoke into the body of the dead marine.

His wounds started to knit almost immediately.

The dead marine looked confused as he gazed about. Maybe the poor guy was just figuring out now that he really was dead. But then he looked at Heath, and the smoke, and realized that his wounds were healing.

"How are you... I mean, thank you." He came to attention. "And thank you for that ... blessing. It kind of woke me up, if that makes any sense."

It did, but Heath didn't want the dead marine to focus on what that blessing meant. Not yet.

"Thank *you*," Heath said. "You saved my life."

"He ambushed you," the dead marine said, frowning. "You sounded to me like you really didn't want to fight, but you weren't going to back down before a bully. You weren't going to cough up the guy who came to you for help." He pointed at Papa Dusk. "Then that jerk tried to flat out *murder* you."

The dead marine shook his head in wonder.

There were a number of things Heath could have said then. He could have admitted that he hadn't been ready for this kind of fight. That he'd been expecting a scout, not the army itself. That if he'd been ready, maybe...

None of that mattered.

But before Heath could speak, the dead marine kept talking.

"Man," he said, taking in more and more of the incense, "that stuff feels good. Why does smoke feel so good?"

"It's an incense that's very healing to the spirit. I tend to keep some with me these days, just in case."

"I'm dead, aren't I?"

Heath nodded. "Sorry to be the one to tell you."

"Is this the afterlife?"

"No," Heath said with a smile. "No, you've got something more coming to you than hanging out like some memory of your former self. I'd help you along myself, but I'm not the one you want doing it."

"Why not?"

Heath jerked a thumb toward the three approaching across the cemetery.

"One of those guys is a priest. Father Antonio. Since this is a Catholic cemetery, he's the one you want laying you to rest."

"Wow," the dead marine said, and his face went slack with wonder. "He glows."

"Figures," Heath said with a chuckle. He turned and saw that Colin had let Tony and DeAndre catch up, and the three of them weren't more than fifty yards away now."

Then Tony began running. Colin started a moment later, but DeAndre, he must have had his fill of running for the day, because he shook his head and kept walking.

Tony, panting and out of breath, arrived faster than Heath expected. In fact, he beat Colin here.

"Tony," Heath said, and gestured to the dead marine, "this is—"

"A moment," Tony said and crouched over Papa Dusk. Checked for breath. Barked at Heath. "You were just going to leave him here?"

"Man tried to kill me and got eaten by a spirit he'd bound. Not my place to get between a spirit and its vengeance."

"Heath," Tony growled, and started performing CPR.

"How long has he been like that?" Colin asked, softly enough that Tony might not have been able to hear over the intensity of his efforts to save Papa Dusk.

"Couple of minutes maybe?" Heath said, and raised an eyebrow at the dead marine.

"Not sure," the dead marine said. "Time feels ... funny to me right now."

Colin focused on the dead marine.

"You're not a ghost," he said with a frown. "You're not supposed to be here."

"Just died," Heath said. "Hasn't moved on yet, but he will. Might need Tony's help."

Tony was still compressing Papa Dusk's chest and trying to breathe life into the old man when DeAndre arrived.

"Shit," he stage whispered. "You killed him? Boy, you do earn your pay, don't you?"

"I didn't do it," Heath said. "I just freed a nature spirit he'd bound as a combat monster."

Colin whistled, soft and low.

"Turned on him, huh?" DeAndre muttered. "Couldn't happen to a meaner guy."

"So he really was evil?" the dead marine asked, like the question was important. "I mean, he had this darkness about him, but I just thought that the sunlight was fading."

That was the moment the sodium lights kicked on, bathing the parking lot in a yellowish light.

"Believe it," Heath said. "That man sacrificed at least one human being to a demon."

"Judge ... not ... lest ye ... be judged," Tony said, while continuing compressions.

"Never did understand that one," Heath said with a shrug. "I get judged all the time. By that logic, I'm *entitled* to judge people."

"Heath," Tony said in a low, warning tone, then breathed air into Papa Dusk's lungs.

Colin shook himself as though just realizing something. He whipped out his phone. Heath saw him hit the number nine then covered the phone with his hand.

"I had to plow into that old bastard with my shoulder," Heath said. "You're calling the cops, I won't be here when they arrive."

"We don't need the police," Tony said, sitting back. "We need an ambulance."

Sure enough, Papa Dusk was breathing on his own.

Before the ambulance arrived, DeAndre collected a little hair, a little skin, a little saliva and a little blood from Papa Dusk. Heath had been willing to do what needed to be done, but DeAndre wanted to handle that part himself.

Of course, Tony almost didn't allow the collecting of those important, personal links. He stood guard over Papa Dusk and demanded that DeAndre swear, under the light of the Archangel Michael, to tell the truth of what he would do with those little bits of Papa Dusk.

Heath was impressed that DeAndre didn't hesitate to answer. Didn't try to fight that compulsion at all. And what he said he'd do was equally impressive in its restraint.

He was going to bind Papa Dusk against working any kind of magic. No magic of root and herb, no magic of will and spell, no magic of spirit or even demon.

That was a use Tony approved of.

And so while DeAndre collected what he needed, Tony took a moment to lay that poor dead marine to rest.

Heath had been hoping to see the dead marine ascend a ladder of lights, or a stairwell, or even an elevator. Something showy to his spirit eyes, that might give Heath some assurance of where that marine's soul was bound.

But the dead marine just faded away as Tony recited his mass for the dead.

Heath hung back around the Lexus while the ambulance was taking care of Papa Dusk. Good excuse for Heath to clean up the tricks Papa Dusk had left behind.

And Heath had been right. They were all around the vehicle, plus on each door handle, as well as the latches of the trunk and hood.

But finally the ambulance was gone, and Heath, Colin, Tony and DeAndre were alone in the yellow light of the cemetery parking lot on that cool September evening. Cool enough that Heath would have liked something more than his light shirt and cargo shorts, but he refused to start shivering. It was a matter of principle.

"I took the blame for the chest bruising," Tony said to Heath. "Said it was part of my efforts at CPR."

"Thanks," Heath said.

"Private Emerson told me to take it easy on you," Tony said, and

Heath presumed he meant the dead marine. "Said you tried hard to avoid the fight in the first place. Also said you felt the nature spirit had its right to vengeance."

"Yep," Heath said. "I work with plenty of spirits. But I invite them. I don't force them."

"You still should have tried to save his life."

"That," Heath said, "I'm less sure of."

"I think you played it right," DeAndre said. "Bastard deserved to die."

"Not your place to say," Tony said, rounding on DeAndre. "Who are you to decree who lives and who dies?"

"That old..."

Heath lost the thread of DeAndre and Tony's argument, because Colin was looking at Heath with one eyebrow raised.

And Heath knew exactly what Colin meant by that.

DeAndre was agreeing with Heath. *DeAndre.* What did that say about the rightness of Heath's cause?

"You're right, Tony," Heath said. He wasn't a hundred percent sure of that, but right then and right there, it felt more important to Heath to agree with Tony as opposed to DeAndre.

And what Heath said next felt more comfortable anyway. It was telling the truth in a way that let the listener draw his own conclusions.

"Truth is, when I saw Papa Dusk hit the ground with his eyes stuck open like that, I figured he was already dead."

Heath shrugged.

"You could still have checked," Tony said.

"I don't know CPR," Heath said. "Only thing I could have done would be to call nine-eleven. And I didn't have a good answer about the bruise to his chest, so I probably would have spent the night in jail. Maybe more than a night, if I didn't get a chance to whip up a little mojo to keep my fat out of the fryer."

Tony frowned at that, but let it go.

"Guess your job's done," DeAndre said with a broad smile. "And you do good work. We'll stop at an ATM and I'll get you the balance of what I owe."

Heath raised his eyebrows. After all, DeAndre had paid in advance, as agreed.

"Figure you deserve a combat-pay bonus," DeAndre said with a smile.

"DeAndre," Tony said, and he didn't sound irritated anymore. He sounded serious though. And he waited until he was sure he had the big man's full attention before he continued.

"DeAndre, you said some things earlier that implied you might be interested in joining my order."

"I would," DeAndre said, "as long as I don't have to take a priest's vows to do it."

Colin snickered at the implications, but everyone ignored him.

"I can ask Brother Theodopolis if you like," Tony said with a pull to his lips that suggested he thought that was a bad idea. "I'll tell you though, you won't even be considered."

"Why, because I'm..." DeAndre flared his nostrils in a quick, deep breath. "Why not?"

"You have committed the mortal sin of murder. You do not repent that sin. Without repentance, there can be no forgiveness. Without forgiveness, there can be no absolution. Without absolution, that stain remains on your soul, an open wound inviting spiritual infection. A member of our order with such a weak point would be a constant danger to himself and to all of the order."

DeAndre blinked. Nodded. "I understand."

"In fact," Tony said with a grimace, "much as I hate to discourage your newfound zeal to battle demons, I strongly suggest you do not do so until you deal with this spiritual wound."

"You said I'm probably going to get arrested for the murder of that guard," DeAndre said, and Heath frowned as a little detail occurred to him. He kept it to himself as DeAndre continued. "Maybe if I do, the time away will give me a different perspective on it."

"Regretting being caught is not the same as repenting the sin."

"I know," DeAndre said, and shook his head. "But right now, I'm still not sorry I did it."

"I understand." Tony shook DeAndre's hand, then gave Colin and Heath each a hug goodbye.

Heath, Colin and DeAndre got back into the Lexus while Tony began making his way back to his monastery.

Heath waited. He waited until they were strapped in and all the doors were closed. He waited until the engine fired up and DeAndre began to drive. In fact, he waited until DeAndre stopped at the ATM to get Heath's bonus, which was not inconsiderable.

Only then did Heath say, "DeAndre, we both know you're no longer barred from affecting legal matters with your magic."

"True," DeAndre said as he drove through the streets of Lake Oswego.

He didn't say anything for a minute, but Heath waited. He had the feeling more was coming.

It wasn't until DeAndre got onto I5 heading back into Portland that he finished his thought.

"I'm not going to mess with this. Maybe if I get arrested. Go to court. Maybe even see the family of that guard, praying for me to get locked away for life. Maybe then, looking at their pain, maybe I'll be able to regret what I did. Repent it, like Father Tony said."

DeAndre turned his eyes to the road ahead. "Maybe that's what I need."

EPILOGUE

An hour later, Heath was home and settled. He'd let DeAndre drop him off at Powell's — no reason to let DeAndre know where Heath lived, he wasn't ready to trust him *that* far — then Colin dropped Heath off at home.

He lay flopped on his bed, with his tuxedo cat Dr. John curled up and purring on Heath's chest, when Nariko's daily call came.

Heath answered, immediately going to video chat.

Nariko was in a tent, so she was still out at Mount Hood. Her lovely face was dirty, with runnels carved in the dirt by sweat that had dried a good hour ago, at least.

But she was smiling, from the corners of her sweet lips to her jade eyes. Her waterfall of black hair had been tied back in a bun, held in place with her trademark steel spike.

"You hung up on Mom?" Nariko said, laughter in her voice. "Oh, tell me all about it, baby. Tell it nice and slow."

"If we're having phone sex," he said, "I don't want your mother in the conversation."

"Fair point."

"So how are things going out there?"

"Good. I might be able to wrap up in a couple of days and be home by the weekend."

"Hope so," Heath said, voice teasing. "I made gumbo. If you aren't home by the weekend, there may not be any left."

"I'll be there," Nariko said, laughing. "I'll be there."

"See, Dr. John?" Heath said, turning to phone to put his cat on camera. "The stomach isn't just the way to a *man's* heart."

Nariko cooed to Dr. John until he opened his eyes and blinked at her, tail twitching in a plain admonition that whatever she was doing was not nearly enough to keep her away from where she should be — on the bed, with Heath and himself.

"Gonna tell me what you're doing yet?" Heath asked.

"Can't," Nariko said, getting serious so fast the change was disturbing. "Right now Mom can't find me. But if I say what I'm doing, she'll hear it. If I even imply what I'm doing, she'll catch enough to figure it out. That's a confrontation I'm not ready for."

"You know I'll be with you when it comes."

"I know it, baby," she said with a warm smile. "Now tell me about your day."

Heath did, and he enjoyed the slack-jawed amazement he got from Nariko when he explained that it had been *DeAndre McDaniels* he'd been helping, and the various things he'd had to do to help the big man.

When Heath finished, Nariko said, "Think he's serious about wanting to bury the hatchet between you two? You could use to knock a name off that long enemies list of yours."

"I don't keep a list," Heath said, "but I'm pretty sure he means it. He wants to get together for a beer down in Tualatin next week. Someplace we can sit and chat without the whole community knowing."

"You'll take precautions, just in case?"

"You know," Heath said, "I *have* managed to live this long."

"Yes," Nariko said, getting a teasing tone as she finished, "but you're dumb in all the wrong ways."

That was the crack Heath had been waiting for. He told Nariko what he charged DeAndre for today's work.

She whistled.

"All right," she said, nodding, "I have to admit. You didn't under-charge for once. Maybe you are learning."

"And maybe," Heath said, deliberately unbuttoning the top button of his shirt, "it's time we stopped talking about your mother and DeAndre and started talking about something more interesting."

Heath popped the second button on his shirt.

"Why, Mr. Cyr," Nariko said as she pulled the spike out of her hair and shook her long hair loose, "I believe you're trying to seduce me."

"Do you have a problem with that?"

"Uh uh," she said, reaching for the hem of her own long-sleeved tee shirt.

And from there, the conversation got far more enjoyable for both of them.

The day may have started too damned early, and yes, it led to Heath coming closer to dying than he liked to think about, but at least it ended on a high note.

SIGN UP FOR STEFON'S NEWSLETTER

Stefon loves to keep in touch with his readers, and loves to keep you reading. The best way for him to do both is for you to sign up for his newsletter.

Sign up at http://www.stefonmears.com/join

If you sign up for Stefon's newsletter, you get...

- Monthly updates about his publishing and travel schedules
- His latest news, in brief, and answers to reader questions
- A free short story for signing up
- List-only offers and occasional specials
- Plus a free short story every month!

ABOUT THE AUTHOR

Stefon Mears prefers reading runes to reading any kind of cards. Stefon has more than thirty books to his credit, and he never stops writing. He earned his M.F.A. in Creative Writing from N.I.L.A., and his B.A. in Religious Studies (double emphasis in Ritual and Mythology) from U.C. Berkeley. He's a lifelong gamer and fantasy fan. Stefon lives in Portland, Oregon, with his wife and three cats.

Look for Stefon online:
www.stefonmears.com
himself@stefonmears.com